Pippa

Annie Seaton

Pentecost Island
1

DEDICATION

To girlfriends all over the world.

Chapter 1

Pippa

'Babe, can you pay the electricity bill today in your lunch hour?' Darren shook my shoulder as I snuggled into the pillow.

I lifted my aching head as I came out of the realms of sleep. I tried to blink, but my eyes were watered with the strong-smelling gel he insisted on using.

'Shit, what time is it?' I put my hand to my eyes as I sat up. My head throbbed, and my nose was blocked.

'Eight-fifteen. You'd better hurry up.'

'Why didn't you wake me up? You know I was supposed to go in early today.' My throat hurt so much the words came out croaky. We'd got home late last night, and I blamed my scratchy throat on too many drinks, and Darren smoking beside me all night.

'Oh, sorry. I forgot you've got that big thing to do today.'

'Yes, the presentation to the new advertising firm.'

He nodded with a smile before he moved to the mirror and combed his hair. 'And that's going to mean another big pay rise for you?'

'I hope so.' A ripple of dissatisfaction niggled through me. All he seemed to worry about lately was how much my next pay rise was going to be. To be honest, I was getting a bit sick of it, but in my usual way I didn't want to rock the boat, so I didn't say anything. I'd picked up the bar tab last night too.

Darren was always chasing deals. He was a freelance finance consultant, and the next big deal was always around the corner. Trouble was, it hadn't arrived yet.

I was starting to realise that what Darren said and what actually happened were two very different things.

I frowned as he picked up the can of gel and sprayed his hair again. He might be good looking, but he worked hard at creating the image of a man around town—as well as spending what I earned to keep that image going. I had to get this pay rise, things had been getting a bit tight lately with him rarely contributing to our joint bills account. Tam and Nell both disliked Darren, and that had meant I'd seen a bit less of them over the past twelve months.

'A user,' Tam said.

Nell shook her head. 'And a loser.'

I loved my friends and I was

sad that we had drifted apart lately. We were all busy in our various careers. Tam was a chef at one of the posh restaurants on the coast, and Nell was an accountant, and even though we lived close by, there hadn't been much socialising lately. Not with them anyway. Darren and I were out every night of the week.

But I knew if we met up with the girls for coffee or drinks, I'd be tempted to dump my relationship dissatisfaction on them and that would be disloyal to Darren.

'Where are you going today?' I swallowed and my throat felt like razor blades were lodged in there.

'A couple of meetings and then a business lunch.' He turned to look at me. 'You look like shit, babe.'

'Thanks. I don't feel very well. Can you grab me a glass of water and a couple of Panadols, please?'

A couple of minutes later he was back and handed me a glass of water and two tablets.

'Thanks.' I swallowed them and drank the whole glass of water. 'I thought you were paying the bills yesterday. What about the car rego?'

'I was a bit short. I picked up the tab for the lunch with the guys from the car dealership.'

'How much was that?' I'd handed over five hundred dollars in cash yesterday morning for the bills. 'What about your business credit card?'

'I maxed it out, and I needed cash for the balance at the restaurant.' He had the grace to look sheepish.

'The balance? Bloody hell, Darren. How much was lunch?' I took a deep breath and my chest hurt.

'Don't stress, babe. This deal should be signed off tomorrow. I'll pay you back once I get my card paid off. This new project Jazz and I are working on needed a little bit more cash for the advertising campaign.' He leaned down and brushed his lips across my forehead. 'Have you got any cash?'

Advertising campaign? A boozy lunch?

He must have seen the look on my face, and he put his hands up. 'It's okay. I just need some petrol. No more business lunches, this week. I promise.'

'This week?' I shook my head, and even that hurt. 'There's two fifties in my purse. Take them.' I sank back into the pillow. 'I'll let the Panadol kick in, and then I'll grab a shower and get out of here.'

'Put lots of makeup on. You

really do look like shit.'

'I love you, too.' I held his gaze, not able to stop the sarcasm in my voice, but he looked away. The way I felt this morning, I didn't care about much at all.

'Honesty. You always say it's important,' he replied as I got another brief kiss on the top of my head. 'But I do love ya, babe. You know that.'

'I do.' Although I wondered about that too lately. There hadn't been much happening in the intimacy department and even before I'd got crook the occasional kiss or hug had been more brotherly than lover-like.

I snuggled back down beneath the doona with a sigh.

Ever since I'd lost my parents and gone to live with Mum's Aunty Vi on Pentecost Island, I'd yearned for a love like my parents had.

Living with Aunty Vi had been interesting . . . and different, but she'd loved me unconditionally. I survived high school on the mainland, staying with one of her friends at Cannonvale through the week, and coming back to the island each weekend.

One thing Aunty Vi had tried to teach me was to be independent and not rely on others so much. She was better than the counsellor I saw at high school, but between the two of them, I don't think they had much success. The counsellor had always called it an acute lack of self-confidence.

Tam and Nell said I had abandonment issues; good friends always tell it how it is, don't they? I knew they were probably closer to the mark. Luckily there had been enough money in Mum and Dad's estate for me to support myself through uni. My two besties had stayed in touch by email in the seven years I'd lived with Aunty Vi, and I guess because it was easier to pour my heart out in emails than it would have been in person; our friendship had never missed a beat, and we picked up where we'd left off when we met up at uni after high school.

Those uni years had been the best years of my life—so far. We pretty much drank our way through the first two years, but the three of us picked up great jobs when we graduated. And as well as my great job in marketing, I picked up Darren.

Although I guess you could say he picked me up. He swept me off my feet at the *Piccolo* bar in the Valley one night just over a year ago and I finally thought I'd found love. I turned my head into the pillow, ignoring the hot tears that seeped from the corner of my eyes.

I don't have time to feel sorry for myself.

Five more minutes. Then a hot shower and a handful of cold and flu tablets. I had to go to work. My—our—whole future depended on today's presentation. Darren seemed to have no hesitation in treating my income—and bank account—as his. When we moved in together six months ago, we'd started a new joint bank account for bills and stuff like that and were supposed to be putting in five hundred dollars a month each.

With a sniff, I closed my eyes as the painkillers kicked in.
##

The loud music of my phone ringtone woke me. I opened my eyes to bright light streaming through the window and the sound of heavy traffic outside.

I grabbed the phone. 'Hello?' I tried to say but no sound came out.

Clearing my throat—it still hurt like hell—I tried again. 'Hello?'

'Pippa, where the fuck are you?' Eric's voice was loud.

'I've got the flu.' I coughed not to make myself sound genuine, but because I could barely breathe.

'You'd better be close by because Clarissa has just got coffee for the advertising guys to stall them. How far away are you?'

I sat up and swung my feet over the side of the bed. I knew I wouldn't be going anywhere when the room spun, and my head thudded. I reached for a tissue on the bedside table and wiped my streaming nose before I answered him.

'I'm still at home. I just woke up.'

'What the fuck? You have to get here, Pip! You've got ten minutes max. Do it.'

'I'm dying. I can't even stand up.' The room was spinning like a merry-go-round and a Ferris wheel rolled into one. 'I'm sorry, Eric, I was coming in, but I went back to sleep.'

'Such dedication. Fucking hell, you know what this means to us?'

'I know. Don't stress. I've done all the work. It's in my PowerPoint.' As much as I hated to say it, I closed my eyes and took a deep breath. 'The presentation is in the shared drive on the network but it's password protected.'

'Right, Clarissa can do it then. She's blonde and she's got boobs. That might make up for her lack of smarts.'

I gritted my teeth.

Why did I surround myself with sexist men?

'What's the password?' he snapped out.

Even though I had a temperature, more heat ran up my neck as I gripped the phone. 'Darren for me. Darren with a capital D, underscore, the number four and then me.'

'Jesus,' he said. I could almost see the eye roll.

'Tell Clarissa she'll be fine. Just tell her to stick to the slides, and you can answer any questions.' Saying those words was one of the hardest things I've done in my life. I wasn't going to beg but I wanted to remind Eric this presentation was the culmination of two months of bloody hard work and lots of research, and I had done it singlehandedly. 'And Eric, just remember no matter how good she puts it across, it's *my* work.'

'I know that. But Pippa? *You* remember if we don't get this contract, you're out of a job. The blame will be squarely at your feet.'

Chapter 2

Pippa

Blasted flu.

If I had to get sick, I couldn't have picked a worse day if I tried. My typical bad luck and surprisingly, not a hint of pink in sight.

Some people have problems with black cats and walking under ladders. Aunty Vi had a phobia about spilling salt, and God forbid, if you ever put shoes on the table in front of my mum, life was not worth living.

My bad luck omen is pink. Not Alecia Beth Moore—the rock star— but pink, the colour. Although if I'm honest, I must admit the time that Tam and Nell wanted me to go to the Gold Coast to see Pink I *was* a bit reluctant, but in the end, I agreed, and it had been a great concert.

No accidents, and no dramas.

That was back in the days before Darren.

Pink—the colour, and Darren have been life changers for me.

It all started at the swimming carnival the year I was in Grade Five. If there was one thing, I hated then, and I still do almost twenty years later, it's diving head first into water. That's how I became the school backstroke champion in Grade 4. You start the backstroke race already in the pool and you don't have to dive into the unknown.

I wonder what a psychologist would have to say about that?

The Fairlands State School swimming carnival was always held on the last Friday in January when the new school year began after the long and lazy summer holidays.

I was one of those nerdy kids who loved school. I guess the time I spent learning new things—and I had a huge thirst for knowledge—made up for the parts of my life that were lacking. Although in my pre-teen years, I didn't realise anything *was* lacking. I didn't know any better until I went to live on the island with Aunty Vi.

I loved that first week of school so much: empty exercise books ready to be filled with sums and stories and neatly covered with crisp brown paper, new pens and pencils, and a brand-new lunchbox. Everything was new and glitzy before chaos took over again.

The only thing that ruined that week for me was those coloured pencils. I always began the school year with a big flat tin of coloured pencils. God knows where Mum got them. Everyone else had textas, but Pippa Carmichael had to have the Derwent coloured pencils from Mum's stash from God knows way back when. *No one* had tins of pencils in 1999. No one else had even *heard* of them.

My mum had been a hoarder. She was different to my friends' mums and she was the person who began my run of 'pink' bad luck.

God rest her soul.

As a child, I often wondered if I hadn't worn pink to the airport that day, if Dad would still be alive. That year he'd gone away on Boxing Day and was due back at the end of the first week of the new school year.

I was determined to beat Jill Hurley in the fifty-metre backstroke. Until the year before Jill had won *every* race *every* year; her parents managed the local swimming pool, and all she ever did was swim laps up and down Yeronga pool. They even made her train before school. I used to feel sorry for her with her chlorine-green hair that looked like clumps of straw by recess every day; she copped a bit of bullying about her hair, but it didn't seem to bother Jill, because she was the school champion.

In Grade 4, I beat her in the backstroke event, and that saw my entry into the friendship group that still includes me today. Well, before Darren, anyway.

Tam and Nell came up to me after the race and high-fived me as I clutched the blue first place ribbon to my flat chest.

'Way to go, Phillipa,' Nell had said with a wide smile.

'It's Pippa,' I said shyly. 'Or Pip.'

'Well done, Pippa,' Tam pointed

across the pool. 'Do you want to come and sit with us?'

I'd followed them to the grassy corner at the end of the grandstand, and a friendship was born that day. I'd only been at the school for a year and a half and up until then I'd been quite happy to sit and read in my lunch hour while the other girls played softball.

I was used to being alone and didn't mind it. Fairlands State School had been the third one I attended in my first four years at school. Mum had always been a bit of a gypsy, and I knew she hated the big two-storey house that we'd moved to in the flash suburb of Fairlands. Dad had bought it for her when I was nine, and I was too shy to try to make friends with the kids who played in the street after school. I preferred to have my nose in a book.

The other problem was Dad and Mum weren't married, and that set me apart at that swish suburban school in Brisbane. Most of the mothers in our street were lawyers or had some sort of high-powered job—and had husbands, house cleaners and gardeners — and the kids had nannies. It wasn't the right sort of street for us. I had Mum—a stay-at-home Mum, and a Dad. When he was there.

Don't get me wrong. Dad was my *real* dad. It's just that my parents hadn't ever got married. Dad didn't care either way, although I think he would have liked Mum to have been Mrs Brody but she didn't believe in marriage. Once I came along—and you have to laugh at this—I think she decided she didn't believe in kids either. But for some reason, she'd insisted that I took her surname when I was born. I've never figured out why, and Aunty Vi had just shrugged when I asked her.

It sounds like I didn't have a lot of respect for my Mum, but for the twelve short years of my life I had a mother, I adored her. We spent a lot of time home alone because Dad worked down on the oil rigs in Bass Strait; he was one of the first fly-in-fly-out workers before it became commonplace.

"Blue collar worker, and not married," I heard Tabitha Stevenson's mother say one day with a sniff when I was in Year Four. I could never figure that out, because as far as I could see, Dad didn't own one shirt with a blue collar.

But one thing I figured out very early. Mum loved him more than she loved me. But I could cope with that because Dad loved me too, but when he died in an accident on the oil rig Mum's heart broke, and I wasn't enough to fill the gaping hole in her life.

I had a gaping hole in mine too, but I had to cope, especially when that hole exploded a few months later.

But I was telling you about the swimming carnival.

Because Dad worked on the rigs he was away for a month at a time. Thirty days on, and thirty days off, so it was pretty special when he came home.

Mum would get herself all glammed up. And I'd always get a new dress to wear to the airport.

The last time Dad came home to us was the end of January 1999, when I was eleven-years-old.

When I looked at the calendar on the fridge and saw the big *pink* heart that always indicated the day of Dad's return, my stomach sank. He was coming home on the Friday of the swimming carnival.

Going to the airport to meet Dad was important, but so was keeping my status of senior backstroke champion of Fairlands State School. I'd trained all holidays and didn't want to miss out on it. Tam and Nell and I had spent the summer holidays at the local pool. They were starting to look at boys, but I was focused on my backstroke.

I walked out onto the front porch where Mum was reading a letter. She looked up at me with a smile and held it up. 'Aunty Vi has invited us up for a holiday.'

'Who's Aunty Vi?'

'My great aunt. She lives on an island up in north Queensland.'

For a moment I forgot the swimming carnival. 'Are we going

to go?'

'We'll see.'

I was used to that. That meant no, it wouldn't happen. Ever.

'She says to tell you how proud she is of you.'

'Me?' I screwed up my nose. 'She doesn't even know me.'

'But I write and tell her all about you. She knows how hard you work at your school work, and how clever you are.'

I shrugged. What an old lady in another state thought about me didn't impact on my life.

'Mum?'

She looked at me over her half-glasses, and as always, I was struck by how beautiful my mother was. No wonder Dad loved her so much; she could have been a movie star. The only thing I got from Mum was her hair colour. Not red, but a sort of pale ginger. She had fair skin like Snow White, but I'd inherited Dad's olive skin and green eyes. It wasn't until I was older that I realised what a strange combination that was.

'Yes, Pippa?'

'What time does Dad's flight arrive?'

'Five o'clock. We'll go after school. I don't want you missing a day of school.'

Yes! Relief ran through me. I was determined to keep the blue ribbon for backstroke. I hadn't even mentioned it to Mum. She didn't come to the school, and she didn't ever do tuckshop. And I don't think she'd even noticed the ribbon stuck to the side of the dressing table mirror for the past year. If she had she'd never said anything.

Like I said, she loved me—I think—but she wasn't one of those school mums that those things were important to.

The week before Dad came home every second month, there was always a mad flurry in the house. The rooms all smelled like furniture polish and baby violets filled tiny little vases on every space. The kitchen benches were covered with fresh-baked bikkies and cakes cooling on wire racks.

I loved that week because the rest of the time, we lived in chaos and made do with bought biscuits and takeaway food.

A bit like Darren and I do now.

I guess I did get more from Mum than the ginger hair.

The morning of the 1999 Fairlands State School swimming carnival dawned clear and sunny. The air was still and sultry, a typical Brisbane summer's day. Anticipation curled in my tummy as

I packed my black togs and towel into my school port.

When I looked out my bedroom window, my only wish, apart from winning the race, was that the afternoon storms would stay away until Dad's plane landed safely. When I headed down to the kitchen, there was no sign of Mum.

I was sitting with my nose in my book eating my WeetBix when Mum called me from the bathroom down the hall.

'Pip, come here, sweetie.'

'Coming,' I called as I wolfed down the last spoonful and put my book aside.

When I walked into the bathroom Mum pulled out a packet of bobby pins. I was the only girl in my class who knew what they were.

'You washed your hair last night, didn't you?' She opened the packet.

'Yes, Mum.' I looked at the bobby pins as worry curled in my stomach.

No, please God, no. Not today.

She picked up a water bottle. 'Come over here.'

'What for?' I scowled, and then quickly got rid of it. I would do what Mum wanted.

I always did.

I knew it wouldn't take much for her to stop loving me, so I was a model child no matter what rebellion festered inside.

I guess that set up the adult I grew to be. I hated confrontation, and I turned a blind eye to some of the things that Darren did that really bothered me.

The counsellor that Aunty Vi sent me to on the mainland told me I craved love and didn't want to risk losing it. He was talking about

Mum, but I guess the pattern had continued with Darren.

'Seeing you washed your hair last night, I'll only have to dampen it with the spray.'

I looked down at the bobby pins she'd tipped into the pretty pink-flowered bowl on the side of the vanity. 'Why?'

'I found you the prettiest pink dress to meet Dad tonight and I want your hair in curls.'

Found? I knew what that meant. In one of the trunks in the shed.

'I have to go to school soon.'

'It's okay. I've got a matching pink scarf to cover the bobby pins,' she said. 'You'll have to wear the dress to school, because I'll pick you up before the bell goes and we can go straight to the airport. Now lean forward. I'm going to try something new.'

Long story short; it was the worst day of my life until the day Dad died.

My togs and towel stayed at home, and I avoided everyone—even Nell and Tam—and sat up in the back corner of the grandstand in the second back row, in the bloody stiff pink shiny dress, and I watched Jill Hurley race home to take first place in the senior backstroke race.

'Fancy sending a child to school like that,' one of the mothers sitting behind me said in a loud voice. I sat still and straight.

The pink scarf Mum had wound around the forty or so bobby pins that were creating ginger kiss curls over my head didn't stop the hot sun burning into my scalp where the scarf didn't quite meet.

'Disgraceful, but what else would you expect? The mother's

not quite right in the head.' I wasn't surprised to hear Mrs Stevenson chime in.

I buried my head in my book as embarrassment made me feel like vomiting.

##

The plane was late, and the thunderstorms were rolling in when my long and lanky Dad walked into the arrival hall at Kingsford Smith Airport. He swept Mum into a hug and kissed her just like they did in the movies.

'Pip, you look gorgeous,' Dad said as he turned to me and lifted me high, even though I was eleven and too big for that. The stiff fabric of the dress crackled as he kissed my cheek. 'Don't worry, darling. I know Mum dressed you up, but you look beautiful. When you get home how about you get your togs and we'll go for a swim down the pool?' He lowered his voice and whispered in my ear. 'After I eat all the yummy things I'm sure Mum's been cooking all week.'

He knew my mother so well. And they loved each other so much. My heart broke when Dad was killed and then when Mum died six months later and I went to live with Great-Aunty Vi, I didn't think I'd ever be happy again.

It took a long time.

'I missed you, Daddy.' My voice was quiet, but he'd already turned back to Mum.

Okay, so my hair might have been in pretty curls when we met my father that night and the shiny stiff pink dress that Mum said was made out of something called taffeta might have looked okay, but I was devastated.

I had another year to wait until I could try for the race again.

But twelve months later I was at school in another state and didn't care about winning a stupid race.

I didn't care about anything.

But worse than not being in that race, that day I knew, somehow, as I traipsed along behind them, that even though I was in their presence, I wasn't as important to my parents as they were to each other.

I've never worn pink again.

Chapter 3

Pippa

As I eased my aching body into the hot bath water, steam tickled my blocked nose and for a brief second, I was able to inhale before it clogged again. Agitation filled me and I clenched my hands as I thought of the presentation that Clarissa, my assistant, would be in the middle of giving.

The presentation that would give me a good chance of promotion. As the lavender-scented water covered my shoulders I reached for the face washer and the bottle of eucalyptus oil and dabbed a few drops on the cloth before I put it over my sore nose.

A measure of calm descended as the pungent smell cleared my sinuses and I could breathe through my nose again. I laid my head back and tried not to worry. There was nothing I could do, and I knew that the presentation I'd prepared was top quality.

The water was warm and soothing, and the second lot of painkillers I'd swallowed while the bath was filling began to take effect. Maybe I could go into the office this afternoon and remind Eric again that it was my work they were using to woo the advertising company. No, my work that they would win the contract with.

Be positive.

That was an affirmation that Aunty Vi had taught me.

The two Ps. Positivity, Pip, she'd say. Over and over again.

Enough times that I'd taken it on board and turned a corner a couple of years after I'd moved to Pentecost Island.

Aunty Vi had been good for me. I closed my eyes as I imagined what she'd say about Darren. She wouldn't be impressed. Maybe I was going to have to rethink that part of my life.

Later. I'd sit down with him when I felt better and tell him that the money train was about to stop. I could do it, and if he didn't like it, he could leave.

It would mean that he didn't love me, and if I really thought about it, I wondered if I did love him. I certainly didn't like our lifestyle. We had to be out every night being seen, although how that was going to help his business, I was yet to find out. I'd sit him down for a talk after the new contract at work was in place.

I lay there in the hot water taking myself through the data, slide by slide, and hoped that

Clarissa was going slowly enough for Eric to add his bit.

I blinked when I heard the front door of the apartment open. Darren was supposed to be in meetings all morning. He wouldn't expect me to be home, and I opened my mouth to call out to him to let him know I was in the bathroom. I quickly shut it when a high-pitched giggle was followed by his deep laugh. I tipped my head to the side, confused, and listened.

Maybe he'd turned the TV on. Another giggle, but this time it was from the hall outside the bathroom.

'No, really, I need to have a shower first, Daz.' The female voice was unfamiliar. 'I'm all sweaty.'

'You'll be even more sweaty soon. Come on, babe, the

bedroom's this way.'

'No, I'm having a shower. You can join me.' The high-pitched voice made me nauseous.

'Okay, we'll start in the shower. There's some really sexy oil in there. I can't wait, babe.'

The impatient tone was one I knew very well. And *my* expensive body oil had been a birthday present from Tam.

Babe!

I sank down in the bath and let the bubbles cover my shoulders and breasts, as disbelief filled me.

What the hell?

The bathroom door opened, but Darren was too intent on the skinny woman in the hot pink underwear to even notice I was in the bath. His lips were attached to hers, and his eyes were closed, but his hands were having no trouble undoing her bra.

My vision was filled with pink underwear.

Bloody pink, of course.

I closed my eyes, opened them and blinked again. This time to a red haze of anger.

You lowlife bastard.

I stared at Darren's hands as they dropped lower, and he pulled her pink G-string down. It was like watching a movie.

But this scene taking place in the bathroom of my apartment was reality and I wasn't going to watch for another second. She was undoing the buttons of his shirt, and I wondered if I was in some sort of flu-induced hallucination. But the cloying smell of Giorgio perfume wafted over as her G-string hit the tiles. So strong, the horrid smell even got through my blocked sinuses. Darren threw his shirt to the floor and turned around to open the shower screen.

I wished I'd had my phone with me. When he saw me lying in the bath, my modesty kept intact by the bubbles, the look on his face was priceless. His mouth opened and his skin went that red mottled colour it did when he played squash. Or had sex.

'Jesus, babe. What are you doing home?' His mouth opened and shut, and the bimbo turned around and squealed. She reached over and grabbed a towel from the rail beside the vanity.

My towel.

'Don't worry, sweetheart.' I was so proud of my calm voice as I lifted a casual hand and pointed to the bimbo's bare boobs. 'I've seen it all before. But maybe not so saggy.'

'Bitch,' she said as she reached down and picked up her pink bra and G-string from the floor—my floor—because I paid the rent on this place.

She opened the door and it slammed behind her as she disappeared into the hall.

'Better go kiss your girlfriend better, *Daz*,' I said in as cold a voice as I could muster with a sore throat and a blocked nose. 'I've obviously upset her.'

'Babe, it's not what you think.'

'So what was it? And what do I think it was?' My laugh was almost hysterical. 'You were about to screw that bimbo in our bed? No, wait, it's my bed, because I paid for that too.'

'Calm down, Pip. I'm sorry. I made a mistake, you've been so busy lately and all tied up with your fucking presentation. It's the first time, I swear.'

'Is it?' I said remembering back

to an earring I found in the kitchen a few weeks ago. I'd put it in my bag and tried to give it to Nell and Tam, but neither of them had recognised it.

'Get out, Darren. Pack your gear and leave. I'll give you half an hour, and then I'm coming out. If you're not gone, I'll . . .' My lip quivered and I swallowed as my mobile phone rang in the bedroom. 'Get my phone for me on your way out.'

He had the decency to look down as he picked up his shirt and put it on.

'And take Miss Pink with you.' It's a wonder the ice in my voice didn't freeze the bath water.
##

There was no point ringing Eric, I had to see him face to face. Half an hour later, I was dressed and striding down the footpath beside the Gold Coast Motorway. The traffic was loud, and the wind coming off the sea was cold. At least it cleared my head a bit; I didn't feel too bad now, but I'm sure it was the adrenalin charging through my blood that had got me this far. I hadn't worried about dressing in office clothes.

As soon as I read Eric's text message, I climbed out of the bath, dried myself—with a clean towel—and grabbed a pair of jeans and T-shirt. I didn't even brush my hair. My hands were shaking too much—I wasn't sure if it was the flu or bloody rage. Darren was still in the bedroom but there was no sign of the bimbo.

'Babe . . .' he said reaching one hand out to me. 'I'm—'

'Fuck off, Darren. And fast.'

I shoved my phone and keys into my pocket and left the

apartment. Slamming the door didn't make me feel any better.

I was not going to be fired by a text message.

If Eric had something to say, he could say it to my face. As I crossed the driveway of the apartments, the postman dropped some letters into the back of the mailbox. I pulled out my key and tried to insert it in the lock, but I was shaking so much it took two attempts. I pulled out two letters and shoved them in my back pocket and took off for the office.

Clarissa was stepping out of the lift when I entered the foyer of the office building. Joe, the security guard was sitting in his usual chair, and his eyes widened when he looked at me.

I stared back and didn't smile. So yeah, my hair wasn't brushed, my T-shirt was wrinkled, and I looked like shit. I didn't care. I felt like shit, but anger was keeping me energised.

I stabbed at the elevator button and ignored Clarissa who had waited by the lift panel.

'Philippa—' She was crying.

'Not now.' I stepped into the lift and pushed the button for the fifth floor. The doors slid closed to Clarissa's sobs.

Too late now sweetheart. She'd obviously stuffed up.

Joe must have rung Eric, because my boss was waiting for me in the corridor outside the lift bank. Suddenly my energy depleted and my breath caught. I put my hand out and steadied myself on the wall as Eric stared at me.

'You cannot fire me by text message.' My voice was ragged, and my legs were trembling.

Reaction to the situation and the one-kilometre fast walk had set in.

'I can and I did. You lost us that contract.'

'I am sick, Eric. And I did no such thing. I did all the groundwork and if they didn't want us—the company—it wasn't my fault. Maybe you need to look further than blaming me.'

For the past few months, I hadn't been one hundred percent content at E and J Marketing. Eric's focus was different to mine, and I didn't agree with the vision he had for the company. But it hadn't been my place to say. It was his company and he paid my salary. A damn good salary.

'Wait here,' he said tersely. Eric turned and disappeared into the office and I leaned against the wall. Within a minute or so, he came back out carrying a small cardboard box. 'Clarissa packed up your drawer and desk cupboard after she did hers. Your termination pay is in your account.'

'And a reference?' I drew myself away from the wall and stared him down.

'If you insist. I'll email one.'

'And what do you mean before Clarissa packed up her desk? Are you blaming her too?'

'No. I can't afford to keep her on.' His voice was bitter. 'I'll be lucky to keep the company.' He glared at me.

What was it with men that nothing was their fault?

I took the box and turned my back on him as I waited for the lift.

I was out of a job.

I had no boyfriend, and I felt like I was dying.

I walked home slowly and when I pushed open the door of

the apartment, I was relieved to see that Darren had gone. I put the box of my work stuff on the kitchen bench and took the two letters out of my pocket. The first letter informed me that the owner of the apartment had decided to move back in, and I was being given a month's notice.

At least that was the third thing; surely nothing else could go wrong today.

As I glanced at the sender of the second letter, a strange feeling replaced the anger that had consumed me since Darren had shown his true colours with Miss Pink.

Positivity, Pip. I could hear Aunty Vi's voice as I slit the envelope open.

##

'We're coming over. With chicken soup.' Tam's tone brooked

no argument, but I shook my head as I held the phone to my ear.

'No. There's no point. I won't be here. Meet me at the top bar of *Solaris* in an hour,' I said.

'You sound like—'

'Shit. I know,' I finished for her. 'And until I get changed and put some makeup on, I look like it too. Darren told me that when I chucked him out.'

'You what?' Tam squealed, and Nell was obviously in the room because I could hear the glee in Tam's voice as she turned away from the phone. 'She's chucked Darren out.'

'Best news ever!' I heard Nell's voice in the background.

I might not have a job, or a boyfriend, or an apartment, but I did have loyal friends.

'I have news and I have a request, so meet me at *Solaris* in an hour and bring an open mind.'

I was about to celebrate with the last two hundred dollars that lowlife Darren had left in my account. Luckily my termination pay hadn't hit the bank before he'd cleaned out what was in there. But you know what? I didn't give a rats.

The letter I held in my other hand was the fourth life changer for the day.

Chapter 4
Tam

'Do you think Pippa's having a breakdown?' Nell frowned as she outlined her lips with her signature red lipstick. 'I've been worried about her for a while.'

'I hope not. But I know what you mean. She'd slipped back a bit.'

'She's been pretty fragile ever since that lowlife moved in.'

Tam shook her head; she'd thought the same thing but didn't want to say it. 'I always think about her mum when she gets down.'

'Well, she sure didn't sound fragile on the phone. I think she's finally woken up to him. I mean she sounded crook, but there was some life in her voice for a change.' Nell grabbed her purse off the table. 'I'm ready.'

It didn't take Tam long to get ready. Pippa's actions were way out of character, and she was worried about her. She never talked about her mother and what had happened when they were in primary school, but Tam still remembered the day as though it was yesterday. Mr Zagami, the headmaster, had come to the door of the classroom himself, and Pippa had been called out.

Tam's mother had told her that she was too young to go to a funeral, and all Tam could think of was Pippa being there by herself. She and Nell got to see her for a few minutes when her aunt brought Pip back to pack up her things in the house.

It had been an awful few months but as soon as Pip was

settled on the island with her aunt, she and Nell had written to her every week. Her aunt—or great-aunt they found out later—had given her address to Tam's mum. It had taken a few months before they got a reply, but Pippa eventually wrote back to them.

'Are you almost ready, Tamsin?' Nell's call interrupted her thoughts.

'Coming.'

She quickly changed into a dress; if they were going to *Solaris* she'd go vintage.

'Oh, nice,' Nell said when Tam went into the living room. 'Where did you get that?'

'When I went up to Brisbane last week.'

'Looks great.'

Nell had moved in with Tam as a temporary measure between jobs two weeks ago. She'd moved to the Gold Coast from her last position with a well-known accountancy firm in Brisbane and was taking a break from work until she got herself settled on the coast.

'Come on, let's get going. You know Pippa. If we're late, she won't hang around.'

Solaris, the "in" bar in Surfers Paradise, was within walking distance of Tam's apartment. Located on the top floor of a twenty-six-floor apartment block near the main shopping centre, with a rooftop pool and gymnasium, it had become the hang out for the beautiful people of the coast over the past year. Nell and Tam had been there one Friday night when it had first opened; Pippa wouldn't go because Darren was tired or some other excuse he'd come up with. The two drinks had cost them a fortune, and they'd soon moved on to their favourite hotel.

Nell rolled her eyes as they walked along Cavill Avenue. 'Remember the first time we met Darren?'

'How could I forget it. He was so obviously trying hard to impress us.' Tam pushed the button at the pedestrian crossing as the late afternoon peak hour traffic sped by. Her mind was elsewhere. She had enough problems of her own, but she hadn't told Nell yet.

'I've never been wrong when I meet someone.'

'Your instincts are always right. You need to give Pippa lessons. She's had a couple of doozies.'

Eventually the walk light turned green, and they hurried across the road.

'No matter how hard I tried, I

couldn't convince her he was a loser.' Nell shook her head. 'It was so obvious.'

'It was because he showed her a bit of love and attention—a few bunches of red roses, a couple of nights out on the town—and she thought she was in love. Poor Pippa can be so needy.'

'We'll look after her. I wonder what he did for her to chuck him out. And I wonder why she wants to meet us at *Solaris* of all places.'

Tam shrugged. 'I don't know. I've got no idea why she picked there, but I'll tell you one thing. I'll only be having one drink. I'll tell you why now, but don't mention it to Pip. She sounded low enough on the phone.'

'Tell me what?'

'I lost my job this afternoon. I think I'm going to have to move back to Brissie.'

'Oh no. Not when I've just come down to the coast. What happened?'

Tam worked in an exclusive jewellery outlet in the Pacific Fair shopping centre. 'The Werners have decided to retire. They don't want to sell the business. They're closing up shop instead.'

'Oh no. When?

'Three weeks. But they've been good about it. They said they'd give me a couple of months pay. And I'm forever grateful to them for taking me on with no experience.'

Nell nodded. 'Yeah, it was a big shift from head chef at Pepper's to selling jewellery.'

'But a necessary one.' They exchanged a glance. Nell was the only one who knew why Tam had quit her job in the hospitality trade.

The doorman at *Solaris* nodded

at them as they walked through the revolving door and headed for the lift. Tam chewed on her lip, wondering what sort of state Pippa was in, and again wondering why the hell she wanted to meet here. Her stomach dropped as the lift gained the top floor in less than five seconds, and she let out the breath she'd been holding when they reached the top.

The coconut-scented air was cool on her skin and she smiled. Even though it was expensive, it was a quirky bar. Retro design, with bright colours that relaxed you as soon as you walked in.

The bar staff wore Hawaiian shirts in reds and blues, and Malibu boards were suspended from the high ceiling. Surfer music provided a catchy background tune.

'I wonder how they get that coconut smell to pump though the air con,' Nell said as she looked around. 'It's just like being on the beach and walking past someone lathering up.'

Tam had to lean closer to reply. The surfie music got louder as they walked towards the bar. 'I don't know, but I love it. Makes me want to go lie on a beach somewhere. Maybe they put reef oil in the filters.'

Nell laughed. 'We live on the most famous beach strip in the country and how often do we get to lie on a beach?'

'Not often enough.'

It was still a bit early for the after-work crowd, and there were only a few people sitting on the high stools at the bar.

'Looks like we've beaten Pippa,' Nell said looking around.

'Unless she got here first and didn't wait.'

'Nah, she would have texted.'

Tam walked along to the end of the bar. A floor-to-ceiling glass wall provided an amazing view over the ocean. The water was the deep blue of late autumn, and the white surf curled in crisp waves that broke close to the shore. A lone surfer waited for a wave, but the sand was crowded with tourists catching the last of the afternoon sun.

Tam took a deep breath. She'd have plenty of time for walks soon. And to lie on the beach. The last thing she wanted to do was go back into hospitality. She pushed back the frustration that niggled in her chest. She'd enjoyed being a chef—cooking was her first love— but the long and late hours had played havoc with her health. Not to mention the emotional mess she'd got into with Chad. She'd not told Pippa about it; she and Nell had made a pact to keep negativity away from her.

'Hey, Pip.' Nell called out and Tam looked across to the left of the glass window where a row of soft brightly-coloured sofas lined the wall. Pippa was sitting on a red one and Tam smiled.

They had been friends since primary school, and Pip could still surprise them. She was a stunning looking woman who wore her beauty unconsciously; she didn't have a vain bone in her body. Her hair was a pale ginger, and her skin was olive. Green almond-shaped eyes and lush lips set in a heart-shaped face, and a tall fine build set her apart in any crowd.

Not to mention her fabulous sense of fashion. The outfits she put together worked for Pippa, and Tam knew if she were to try to wear the same clothes, she'd look ridiculous with her dumpy figure and curly blonde hair. That's why she wore dresses and kept her hair up.

Pippa spotted them and jumped up. Her retro short culotte set looked like something from the 1940s and her hair was twisted into an old-fashioned French roll, but as Tam got closer, the pink nose and the tired eyes stood out like beacons.

'You look like you need a rum, aspirin and lemons, sweets,' Tam said. 'I'll go get you a Bundy.'

'No. I've already ordered a bottle.' Pippa gestured to the table where a bottle of champagne and three glasses sat on a tray.

'Wow,' Nell exclaimed. 'Moet! Are we celebrating the demise of Darren?'

Pip pulled a face as she flopped

back onto the sofa.

'That's one of the things to celebrate. I should have listened to you two when you told me he was a loser.'

Tam shook her head. 'You had to find it out for yourself. Not worth risking our friendship over.'

'It wouldn't have come to that.' Pippa lifted the bottle and poured the first glass, bubbles cascading over the side. 'You gals always come first with me, you know that.'

'And Darren didn't like that,' Nell said.

'Here, let me do it.' Tam held her hand out for the bottle. 'It's too good to waste.' She looked quizzically at Pippa when she passed the icy bottle over. 'How much did that set you back?'

'Okay, it's bribery. I know how much you pair love your bubbles.' Pippa sat back and folded her arms. 'That bottle, my dear friends, cost me my last two hundred dollars.'

'You're mad.' Tam knew her eyes were wide as she poured the second glass. 'All the more reason not to spill a drop though.'

'What do you mean your last two hundred dollars?' Nell looked at Pip as she took the glass from Tam.

'Darren cleaned our bank account out. And the lowlife must have guessed my password because he transferred money from *my* account too before he withdrew it all.'

'Jesus, Pip.' Tam was indignant. 'What are you going to do about it? See the bank?'

Pippa waved her hand. 'He can have it. It wasn't that much. Most of my money is in a term deposit. It's worth it to get rid of him. At least he withdrew it before my termination pay went in. I've changed my banking password, so he can't get his hands on that.'

'What termination pay?' Tam stared at Pippa.

Pip's eyes were hard and glittering, as she dug a tissue out of her bra and wiped her nose.

'Are you on any meds for that flu? Should you be drinking?' Tam couldn't help herself.

'Stop being mother. I'm a big girl, Tam. And no, just paracetamol. A good night's sleep will fix me up.'

'What termination pay?' Nell repeated Tam's question in a gentle voice.

Pippa leaned back in the sofa and picked up the third glass of bubbles. 'It's been a very interesting day. Where shall I begin?'

'At the beginning, please.'

Pip closed her eyes as she sipped.

Tam lifted her glass and wrinkled her nose when the Moet bubbles tickled.

'First thing was, I woke up with the flu. I went back to sleep when Darren left and when I woke up, I was late for work for my presentation.'

'That big one? The one that was going to set you on a skyrocket trajectory in marketing?' Nell's usually soft voice rose.

'That's the one. I was as crook as, and I overslept, and then Eric rang absolutely peed off. Clarissa did the presentation instead of me. But it did have one good outcome. It meant I was there when Darren brought his bimbo home for a lunchtime romp in my bed.'

'Oh, Jeez, Pip. I'd like to say

I'm sorry, but I'm not.'

'It's all good. As he was leaving, I got a text message from Eric telling me I was out.'

'Out what?' Tam took a swig of her champagne.

'Out of a job. Sacked, fired, *finito*.'

'Bloody men,' Tam said. 'But you've got company, sweets. She looked across at Nell. 'Until Nell picks up a job, that makes the three of us unemployed.'

A smile broke over Pip's face. 'Really. You've lost your job too? That's fantastic!'

Tam pulled a face. 'That's not quite the word I'd use.'

'Oh, I got notice to leave my apartment too. But . . . ta da . . . Pippa reached over and pulled out a letter from her small bag. 'There was one more thing that happened today and it means if you two are prepared to be flexible, I can offer you both a job.'

'A job? What sort of job?' Tam said.

'What do you mean flexible?' from Nell.

Pippa sat back and folded her arms. 'If you could do any job you wanted, anywhere in the world, what would you choose?"

'Trick question?' Tam asked with a frown. Pippa was not usually spontaneous. A decision could often take her a few weeks of deep consideration before it was made.

'No, I want a truthful answer from both of you. Nell?'

'If I could go anywhere? Hmm . . .' Nell tapped her lip. 'It would be somewhere warm. No winter, lots of blue skies, and near the ocean.'

'And the job?' Pippa asked.

'Number crunching, of course. I'd like to be in charge of a

business.'

'Tam, your turn.'

'Easy,' she replied as she stared at Pippa. *What was she up to?* 'I'd have my own restaurant. Same as Nell, no winter, blue skies, and near the water.'

Pippa leaned forward and lifted the bottle, before she topped up the three glasses and bubbles overflowed down the sides of the fine crystal glasses.

'Pip, don't waste it,' Nell cried.

Pippa grinned back at her and then put her glass down before she sneezed. She blew her nose and her voice was croaky as she picked up her glass again.

'I want to propose a toast, but I won't do it unless you both say yes. If I was able to offer you both a job, the perfect jobs that you've both just described, what would you say?'

Tam looked at Nell, and Nell stared back at her before they both turned to Pippa.

Tam was the first to lift her glass. Nothing ventured, nothing gained, even though she didn't have a clue about what Pippa was on about. Nell followed suit.

'Yes,' they said together.

'I am proposing a toast to our new business venture. We have an accountant, a marketing expert, and a top-class chef. Here's to us.' She waited for the others to clink their glass on hers, and then chuckled. 'Okay, now I'll tell all.' She lifted the letter. 'This is our ticket to freedom and achieving our dreams.'

'Come on, Pip, the suspense is killing me.' Tam sat forward.

'Ta da.' Pippa pulled the letter from the envelope and began to read.

'Dear Ms Carmichael, I apologise for the time it has taken to finalise the estate of your great aunt, Violet Daphne Carmichael, but as there is another resident on the island, the ownership of the property had to be carefully established. The surveying has been completed and I am pleased to advise that there are no encumbrances on your property on Pentecost Island, and the deeds are in the process of being transferred to your name, as sole beneficiary of Miss Carmichael's estate.

The estate consists of her house and the western half of the island. The island has been divided evenly, between your portion and the other owner.

I would be grateful if you could call me to organise a suitable time to attend my office in Mackay, and

I will take you through the process of finalising the legal documentation.

Your sincerely.
Charles Morton
Morton and Morton, Mackay.'

'Bloody hell.' Tam stared at Pippa. Her face was flushed, and her eyes had lost their hardness.

'Pentecost Island? Where we spent that holiday with you in Grade Ten? Where you lived with your Aunty Vi?'

Pippa nodded. 'The very same. And the island where we are going to start up our own resort. I have a chef and an accountant. How long before you can pack up and come with me?'

Tam and Nell looked at each other.

'Can we have some time to think about it?' Nell, always the sensible one asked.

'Why? You both told me what you want.'

'But what about the money?' Tam put her glass down on the table. 'Setting up a resort won't be cheap. And if I remember your aunt's house, it wasn't in a very good condition fifteen years ago. What's it like now? And what are we going to live on?' She shook her head. 'Fish and yams? Pip, you've always been a dreamer. Have you really thought this through?'

Pippa nodded. 'I have. And to make your decision easier, I want you both to know that I desperately want both of you to come with me. I *need* you gals with me.' She grinned. 'Who knows, there might be a Darren up there and I'll stuff up again without you to watch out for me.'

Tam shook her head, but she smiled as her interest fired. 'That's emotional blackmail, Pippa Carmichael.'

Pip sneezed again and wiped her nose. 'I rang Mr Charles Morton this afternoon. Not only did I inherit half the island, but Aunty Vi left me a significant amount of money. I'm going to do this properly. You'll both be on a salary while we go up and start work. Planning, renovating and building, and working for ourselves while we create the best resort in the Whitsunday Islands. If you don't want to, I'll hire another accountant, and another chef. And I have to fill a lot more positions eventually anyway.'

Nell was the first to hold up her hand for a high five. 'I'm in.'

'And me.' Tam followed suit and held her hand up. 'Don't think the pair of you are leaving me here by myself.'

They all linked hands.

'What do we say?' Pippa said with a wide grin.

'All for one, and one for all,' they chanted together, and burst into peals of laughter, ignoring the curious looks of the other customers and the barmen.

Chapter 5
A month later
Pippa

Everything went like clockwork. I packed up the apartment, and Tam had no trouble getting out of her lease. Rental accommodation was short on the coast, and the owner was ready to move in as the removalist loaded my furniture in the truck. I'd sold my bed to them; that was one thing I didn't want to take to Aunty Vi's house.

Not that I had much furniture, but between the three of us, we had filled a truck and rented a storage shed at Airlie Beach until we sussed out the state of the house and worked out what we'd need to take over to the island. How to get it there was a problem we'd sort out later. It was going to be hard enough getting us over there; the weekly launch that had taken me to the mainland and returned me to the island when I was at boarding school had stopped running two years ago.

The last time I visited the island was just before that. I sat beside her on the wide front porch that looked down over the bay, and she'd told me she was thinking about moving to the mainland.

'I'll miss that view,' she said. 'It's been a part of my life for over sixty-five years.'

I'd blinked back tears. 'I'll bring you out here for visits if you move.'

'No, once I go, it's for good. If I came back, I wouldn't want to leave. Getting old is a bastard, Pip. I can't see well enough to read any more, and my hips are just about worn out.'

'For eighty-five, I think you're pretty damn good,' I'd retorted so I didn't cry.

'I'm not complaining. I've had a marvellous life, and girl, I want you to promise me that you will too. Take life by the horns and go for it.'

I swallowed as I remembered that conversation. Aunty Vi certainly wouldn't have approved of Darren. I didn't ever see her again. She died the weekend Darren and I moved in together, and I'd told myself it was a bad time to go up.

Besides, she's dead, babe,' Darren had said. 'She wouldn't know if you were there or not.'

No Aunty Vi certainly wouldn't have liked Darren.

Or Brett or Rob before him. At least I hadn't moved in with them.

'I'm going to stay here until I

have to move. If I have to, I'll sell it eventually,' she'd said on my last visit. There's been a few developers after it over the years.' She shook her head. 'But lately so many of our island resorts have closed, and the bloody Chinese are buying the islands. I'd love to see my place turned into a resort, but it won't happen in my lifetime.'

It had only been a few months later that she called me and told me that she had moved to the mainland. Aunty Vi had no close family, and the whole time I'd lived with her, no one had been to visit. Darren and my job had taken all of my focus in those months and I guess I'd just assumed that when she moved away, Aunty Vi had sold up, so when I received the letter from Mr Morton about my inheritance, it had been a shock.

So, my new life—taking it by

the horns—was about to begin. And I was going to follow Aunty Vi's dream. It was the least I could do to make amends.

I was meeting Tam and Nell at the Gold Coast Airport at three o' clock. I had one final look around the apartment, left my keys in an envelope on the kitchen bench and closed the door behind me for the last time. The taxi I'd booked was waiting in the car park at the back of the apartment block, and the driver jumped out and grabbed my two bags. He was a good-looking guy about thirty.

'Going on a holiday, gorgeous?' He gestured to the straw hat I was clutching.

I nodded, ignoring the come-on. 'Yeah.'

I climbed into the back seat, and he talked all the way down the motorway, and I did my best to ignore him, but he was kind of cute.

By the time we got to the airport, I found out he was doing law at Bond University, had just broken up with his girlfriend and was on the lookout for a good time.

He asked for my phone number when I paid the bill, but I shook my head. 'No point, I'm not coming back.'

I learned two things from that taxi ride, and I didn't like the first one.

I was still a sucker for any good-looking guy who put the hard word on me. Just as well Tam and Nell were coming north with me. Despite my age, I still had some growing up to do.

The second thing I realised made me smile. I *wasn't* coming back.

Tam and Nell were at the coffee shop at the northern end where we always met when we were travelling together. Nell was in shorts and a T-shirt, wearing a baseball cap and had her ratty backpack in her hand.

Tam was in the usual retro dress and the bright colour made me smile. The red background had huge yellow poppies printed on it, and the poppies matched her patent leather shoes and matching shiny box handbag. Her blonde curls were held up in a clip. Poor Tam had a thing about her body image. She was curvy and always looked stunning, but she translated that to *fat*. Or chubby. Or dumpy. Whatever her current word was.

After hugging both of them, I shook my head. 'Tam, you do realise that there's no vintage stores where we're going, don't you?'

'I know there's no stores on the island.' She grinned. 'But there are planes that will take me back to the city when I need to shop.'

'Girlfriend, you won't have time to shop,' I said with an answering grin. For the past four weeks, we'd pored over business plans and dreamed and laughed. A lightness had taken over my usual serious nature, and the intense motivation that had driven me to succeed in my marketing career had transferred to this new project.

But this one was all mine, and whether it was successful, or an abject failure would be on my head. Too many doubts about whether this idea of taking life by its horns and going into a new business were starting to fill my head at night.

We flew into Hamilton Island after dark and headed for the hotel where we'd booked three beachside bures. To their credit, both my friends had insisted on paying for their accommodation, and I smiled as I reluctantly agreed. Even though I had a significant amount of money invested to use for the development of the resort, I was being cautious. Until I saw the house on the island, I had no idea what it was going to cost to realise Aunty Vi's dream. We were going to spend a couple of days on the island and check out the local contractors. I'd made some early enquiries while I packed up.

'The repairs from the cyclone a couple of years ago are mostly finished on the island resorts and on the mainland, so I'm hoping that it won't be too hard to get tradesmen to come out to Pentecost,' I said to Nell and Tam as we walked across the foyer after we checked in.

'We're not on the payroll yet,' Tam said. 'This is a little holiday before we start work.'

'And we have to suss the island out before you decide to go ahead, for sure,' Nell, ever the voice of wisdom, added. 'Maybe it will all be too hard, and we'll have a holiday and go back to the Gold Coast.'

'So, until then, we treat it as a holiday, and we pay our share.' Tam nodded.

'Have I told you recently that I love you both?' I said.

Tam shoulder-bumped me as we headed outside, keys in hand. 'That doesn't mean much because you said you loved Dazza too for a while there.'

I bumped her back and grinned. 'But you two have endured longer than anyone. Remember that time in Grade 5 when we all sat on that swing at the gate of the school and we made a vow?'

'Oh God, I'd forgotten all about that.' Nell swung her backpack off and carried it.

Tam nodded. 'Me too. You've got such a good memory, Pip.'

I didn't want to spoil the mood by saying that it was only good because most of my happiness was set in memories. I swallowed and shook away the maudlin thought.

'Yep. We vowed no matter where we were, and what we were doing we were going to get together somewhere exotic on our thirtieth birthdays.'

Nell giggled. 'And we thought thirty was old.'

'I thought twenty was old when I was a kid,' Tam said. Her eyes lit up as she looked at us both, and the huts came into view. 'And hey, we're all going to turn thirty in a few months.'

I spread my hands as we stood looking at the gorgeous grass huts we were about to sleep in. 'Maybe it was a premonition. We have the exotic location at our fingertips. We're already here, gals.'

Chapter 6
Tam

'This is absolutely incredible. I'd forgotten how beautiful it is up here.' Tam stood on the beach in front of the bures. Sapphire blue water dotted with the white sails of boats moving through the channel between Hamilton Island and the big island to the north had been a constant feature of the landscape since she'd walked outside with her first coffee of the morning, and Pippa and Nell had joined her.

'I thought we needed to get a feel for island life tourist-version before we head over to Pentecost and start work,' Pippa said.

Tam had noticed Pippa was on edge when they arrived last night, and she couldn't put her finger on what was wrong. She knew better than to delve too deeply when Pippa went quiet.

Maybe it was the thought of going to the island and knowing that Pip was a shocker at picking partners; this was the third guy who'd let her down. No matter how much Pippa said she was over Darren, Tam knew she was still hurting. Not from breaking up, but from the betrayal.

Then again, maybe it was the thought of the big step they were all taking. It was good that they'd all have their own space in the three huts for a few days; they were going to be living in close proximity on an isolated island for a long time.

Nerves coiled in Tam's stomach as she wondered if she and Nell had agreed too readily. The prospect of what they were going to do was exciting, but the planning and organisation was the part she was worried Pip hadn't given enough thought to.

'Good idea.' Nell's words interrupted her musing. 'Pippa, while I think of it, what's the phone service like on the island? Will we even have service? My mum wanted to know when I called her last night to let her know we were here safely.'

Pippa shrugged. 'I'm not sure. When I lived out there with Aunty Vi, it was before we all had mobile phones. When I last visited, I didn't turn my phone on.' She put a finger to her lips and frowned. 'She had some sort of radio thing in the small room off the kitchen. Do you remember that when you visited?'

Nell shook her head. 'All I remember is exploring the island. It was a long time ago. What about you, Tam?'

'I remember it raining for most of the week we were there, but we spent most of the time outside. I remember the water and the house. But Aunty Vi did let our parents know we were there, so there must have been some form of communication.'

'We'll make some enquiries tomorrow. I think we need to sit down and make a list of things that we can't do without, before we head over on Saturday. The first thing I have to do is find out the best way to get over there. We might have to charter a boat. One big enough to take our stuff over.'

'The ferry doesn't run anymore?" Nell asked.

'No. But once we get to the island, I know there's an old launch that Aunty Vi had. Or there was, and the solicitor did mention it as being part of the estate.'

'Can you drive a boat?' Tam was beginning to wonder if they had gone in too deep, too fast.

'I could when I lived there, but she was an old tub even back then.' Pippa turned away and put her hand up to her eyes. 'Finish your coffee and come for a walk. I saw a track heading along the back of the beach to some more huts when I went for a walk earlier.' She pointed to the east. 'If we walk to that rocky outcrop, we should be able to see Pentecost Island.'

As they walked, Pippa was quiet, and Tam glanced at Nell who nodded slightly.

'Let's get this list sorted while we walk,' Tam said cheerfully. 'Nell, what can't you do without?'

Nell smiled. 'Apart from the givens of food and water'—

Pippa finally smiled. 'And

bubbles.'

'And bubbles,' Nell agreed. 'I guess it's my laptop and internet access. I've got my dongle, but that relies on phone service.'

'Until we get there, I'm not even sure if we have electricity. There were a couple of generators there when I was a kid, but it's all an unknown.'

'What about you, Tam?'

'My cooking tools. Do you think we should go over for a day trip, and check it out, and then come back? I know it's going to be pretty basic—' Tam looked up as Pippa spoke over her.

'No. We'll need to have a few days there, and then once we do that there's no point coming back to stay here. We'll get sorted and then come back over in the launch and get whatever we need. When we're ready, we'll have to get our stuff out of the storage shed and get it over somehow.'

They came to the end of the track. 'Are you up for a bit of bush walking?' Pippa asked.

Nell looked hesitant, but Tam nodded. 'Why not? We're going to have to get used to doing it rough, I think. At least after our walk we can go to the breakfast room and be waited on. I'll bring a pen and my notebook, and we'll make a comprehensive list.'

'And then after breakfast, I'll go down to the marina and suss out some charters to get us out there.' Pip's face had brightened a bit and relief filled Tam. Whatever had been on her mind, it seemed she'd let it go.

'Come on, girls,' she said. 'Let's go exploring.'

They followed a narrow track that led away from the beach. Lush forest surrounded them, and the light was dim as they crossed a small creek of crystal-clear water that ran from the top of the hill behind them to the sea. Brightly-coloured parrots hung from the trees and then suddenly they all flew off squawking in a wave of colour.

'It's pretty,' Nell said. 'And I remember the parrots on your island, Pip.'

Pippa stopped walking. 'Pentecost *was* beautiful, but I want you both to be prepared to see how it might be now. There's been a cyclone through a couple of years back, and there could be damage, but Mr Morton did say the house is intact.'

'How does he know so much about the place? Did he come and have a look?' Tam linked her arm through Pippa's, and they started walking again. The track widened, and a glimpse of blue appeared ahead through the lush foliage.

'I'm not sure,' Pippa said slowly. 'Maybe he got a local to come over?'

'Whatever we find, it's a fabulous adventure, and a challenge, and no matter what we find, we will make it work. I'm already brimming with ideas for an outdoor restaurant on a jetty, and new menus.'

She reached down and squeezed Pippa's hand. 'Pip. Thanks so much for including Nell and me in this. It's a wonderful opportunity. And I know it's going to be lot of hard work, but hey, what a place to do it.'

'Yes. It is going to be hard work and we're all going to learn new skills.' Nell moved to Pippa's other side as they approached the water. 'But when any of us get down, and wonder what we're doing, we'll bring each other up. I'm excited now, but I think we'll probably have some doubtful days.'

The track ended and Pippa ran ahead to the rocks leaving Tam and Nell behind.

'Is she okay, do you think?' Nell asked as she watched Pippa climb the rocks. 'She's been very quiet today.'

Tam nodded. 'She's come out of it a bit. It's just Pippa processing things her own way. As well as our friendship, remember we've both got families to fall back on. Pip's only got us.'

'It's not going to be easy, but we will have to be there for her too. But I'm really looking forward to starting work.'

'Me too,' Tam said. 'Come on,

let's go see if we can find this island.'

They stepped out of the forest into brilliant sunshine. Pippa was way ahead of them, standing on the edge of the rocky headland and looking to the south. Her hand was shading her eyes, but when she turned around as Tam and Nell approached, her lips were wide in a happy grin. She lifted her other hand and pointed to the volcanic plug rearing from the deep blue water in front of them.

'There she is, my lovelies. Pentecost Island.'

Chapter 7

Pippa

We had a quick lunch in a coffee shop near the marina. Tam and Nell were going for a walk along the shopping precinct—all research, they assured me—and I was going down to the marina to make some enquiries. Since I'd seen Pentecost Island across the water I was itching to get there, but we needed to be prepared first.

Over lunch I told the girls what Mr Morton had said. 'I'm not too worried about it, but he reckons we're going to meet some opposition with my plans for the island.'

'Planning stuff, I assume, but that's where we'll do our homework once we get over there. Who knows, we might be remembering an idyllic location

that only lived in our memories,'
Nell said.

Tam gestured to the view
across from the coffee shop. 'Even
with the crowds here and the little
motorised cart things and all the
noise, this is still pretty idyllic.
Look at the colour of that water.'

'And the palm trees with those
hammocks. I think we definitely
need to consider hammocks
between palm trees,' Nell butted
in.

'We have lots to do before
hammocks,' I said with a smile.
'But listen, don't mention to
anyone that we're heading over to
Pentecost Island. I'd like to keep it
quiet for a while, in case there is
any opposition.'

'It's not part of a National Park,
is it?' Tam asked.

I shook my head. 'It never
used to be, but while you're out

and about, can you see if you can pick up maps? And look for some with walking tracks and stuff too.'
##

We needed to purchase the basics, and food and plenty of bottled water—in case the tank was dry at the house—but first, I was on a mission as I set off for the marina. Back in my high school days, I'd made friends with a guy on the ferry that had done the run out to Pentecost Island three times a week. In those days, there had been hikers and birdwatchers who'd camped on the beach, and it was that client base that I had in mind for our resort.

Eco-resort was the term that Tam had come up with as we'd had a coffee before we'd got on the plane at the Gold Coast.

I liked it. And I could already see the advertising possibilities.

Not a low market backpacker type of establishment, but high end with decent facilities rather than basic huts and shared facilities. These days it seemed that there was a higher call for luxury—or maybe that was just me. Research would inform our final decision.

'I'll meet you back at the hotel in a couple of hours,' I said as we left the coffee shop.

The chances of my friend, Jiminy—yes, that was his real name—still being around were pretty slim. The whole dynamic of tourism, and subsequently tourism around the islands, appeared to have changed, according to the brochures I'd read in the compendium in the hut.

As well as reading them, I took some photos of the shopping precinct and the views as I walked slowly down to the marina.

The marina was busy with a variety of vessels coming and going. A small tinnie holding a couple of fishermen motored along the break wall, and a couple of larger rubber ducky tenders came in from catamarans anchored in the bay. A massive superyacht with a US flag on the top sat at the end of one wharf. Tourists milled around eating ice creams and taking photos. A couple of teenagers sat at the end of the first wharf, fishing lines dangling in the water. The island had a happy, peaceful feel to it, less frantic and cosmopolitan than the busy Gold Coast where I'd spent the last ten years.

An unfamiliar relaxation settled in my bones and the usual shaky tingling in my fingers had eased since we'd arrived. Up until I'd lost my job, as soon as one project had ended there had always been another one ahead, with the pressure to perform and make money for the company. My level of stress had impacted on me physically, and if I was honest, it hadn't been good for my mental health either. Pressure had come from home too.

Over the last year when I'd get home, stressed and tired, Darren always wanted to go out and hit the high spots.

'I have to be seen, babe,' he'd say.

Wanker.

Now the only pressure on me would be that of my own making. I had loved my job with Eric, but with the new project, it was all mine and I held control. We'd spend the first few days on the island doing a feasibility study; if it wasn't going to work, well then, there was nothing to worry about. I'd convert Aunty Vi's old house into some sort of comfortable accommodation, and if I didn't go down the eco-tourist resort track, I'd live there while I considered my future.

But I was determined to make it work.

I walked along the main wharf until I came to the end where the ferries had moored over ten years ago. The big barge that brought goods across from the mainland had just departed and two men were loading boxes onto a truck.

To my delight I recognised Jiminy. I waited until he'd loaded a crate onto the back of the truck before I walked across and called out. 'Jiminy! Jim!'

He turned and stared for a moment before a grin crossed his face. Dropping the rope in his hand

Jiminy strode across the wharf to where I waited.

'Well, look what the tide's washed up! Phillipa Carmichael!' He held his arms wide and I stepped in for a hug.

'I didn't expect to see you still working here,' I said kissing his cheek.

'The island is my home. Always will be.' He stepped back and looked at me. Jiminy and I had been great mates back in our school days. He was a few years older than me and had left school to work on the boats when he was in Year 11, not long after I'd started my first year at Prossie High. I'd got to know him when we'd caught the ferry over to the mainland at the end of each weekend for the school week and he'd been kind to a nervous first year high school student. After he'd left school, he'd worked on the ferry on the Pentecost Island run and we'd become good mates. But our friendship went the way of many, and we'd lost contact when I left the island and headed south.

'Wow, look at you, girl! All grown up. Last time I saw you, you were heading off to your last day at Prossie High School.'

'That was well over ten years ago, Jim. I went to uni, got a job and when Aunty Vi moved to the mainland, I had no reason to come out here to the island.'

The other man started the truck and Jim gave him a wave. 'I'll meet you up at the store, Bill,' he yelled across the wharf. The driver nodded and we stepped to one side of the narrow concrete wharf as the truck moved slowly past us.

'I'll walk up with you, and we can have a catch up. How long are you on Hamo for? A holiday?'

I shook my head. 'Sort of. Just a short one. I came down here to find out how I can get out to Pentecost Island these days. I know the ferry doesn't run any more, so I guess it'll have to be a private charter?'

Jiminy walked along beside me. He'd grown into a tall man and was obviously fit. His shoulders were broad, and his skin was tanned, and his face already had that weathered look of the boaties who spent their lives on the sun and water. I guess he'd be heading for his late thirties now.

'You won't be able to go out there, sorry, Phillipa.'

'I go by Pippa—or Pip—these days.' I turned to him with a frown. 'And what do you mean? I know the ferry doesn't go out there now, but has something changed since

Cyclone Debbie? Is it too hard to get into the bay now?'

'No, the new owner has made it a private island. No day trippers allowed.'

'New owner? Private? What do you mean private?'

Jiminy scratched his head. 'I guess because he lives there, and he's discouraged visitors. I don't know that he can say no, but none of the charter boats go out there now.'

I stopped walking and crossed my arms as disbelief hit me. 'Well, I'll be going out there. Have you still got a boat, Jim?'

He nodded. I started walking again and I caught him up.

'You remember Aunty Vi? Where I lived when I was in my teens?'

'Yes, of course I do. She was great friends with my nan when they were in the aged care home at Prossie. I used to see her a fair bit when I went to visit. My nan died last year. Your Aunty Vi was a sweetie.'

'She was. She was also a very private person and didn't want to have a funeral or any fuss or bother but I do feel guilty that I didn't even come up when she passed away.'

Or before, I thought, I didn't say it because the guilt was too raw.

'Life intrudes.'

'It does, but I should have come.'

Jiminy shrugged. 'Maybe. Maybe not. She was gone so would it really have made a difference?'

'I guess not.' What he said made sense, but I should have come up to visit Aunty Vi when she was in care. I used to call her each week until Darren arrived on the scene, and she'd said that she didn't want me to visit, and I knew that she'd meant it. There was no beating around the bush with her, and she was sharp as a tack until her body let her down. I was sad, but Jiminy talked sense. I stopped and put my hand on his arm. 'Tell me about this person who says they own the island.'

The look he shot me was curious. 'I don't know for sure that he owns the island, but he owns a fair chunk of it and he's built a big flash house up on the point. You know, just above that lovely beach with the coral heads at each side of the bay?'

'I know it well. I used to call it Swan Bay. I saw some swans there once when I was first at Aunty Vi's. They reminded me of that story—' I cut off. Telling Jiminy about a fairy-tale that had fascinated me ever since I was a child was irrelevant. 'Bottom line, Jim, Aunty Vi has left me her house, and at least half of Pentecost Island, so he can't own *all* of the island. But please keep that to yourself. I need to find out what's going on.'

'No problem. And that's great news to know that it's yours.'

'I'm considering doing some development out there so I'm very interested to hear what you know about them.'

'Just a him, he's English. He lives on the island alone and is supposed to be a bit of a recluse. And you know what the islands' gossip grapevine is like. All sorts of rumours abound. He's supposed to be a movie star one day, and then a billionaire investor the next. Last I heard he was a famous author, but I've never seen his name anywhere.'

'What is his name?' I asked.

'Rafe Rendell.'

I shrugged. 'Never heard the name either.' But I noted it so I could Google him when I got back to the hotel.

'Since he arrived in the islands a couple of years ago, he's not been receptive to anyone going on the island. All the birdwatching and the climbing has stopped now. I haven't seen a boat there for a long time. I mean you still see the private charters go down that way, but it's not a good place to moor the way the weather blows in from both the south and north so most sailors just keep going down to Shaw Island.'

'So . . . if I want to go out there—' I shook my head — 'I mean when I go out there. We've only booked on Hamo for a couple of days to get some provisions together.' We'd started walking again and reached the edge of the marina and the road was above us; a couple of the electric buggies that tourists used to get around the island whirred past.

'How many of you?'

I shook my head. 'Three of us, and we need to get out to Aunty Vi's. Do you still have a boat?'

Jiminy chuckled. 'Is the Pope a Catholic?'

'Okay, smartie, let me clarify that. Do you have a boat that I can hire for you to take us out to the island on Sunday?'

'Of course, I have. But none of this hiring business. I'll take you out as a friend. Sara and I were talking about taking the kids out this weekend.'

'Sara? Kids?'

Jiminy positively beamed. 'My

wife and two kids, Lola and Baden.'

'Congratulations.'

'Life's been good to me. How about you, Pippa? It's a long time since you left. You said we? Married? Kids?'

I shook my head. 'No, I've been a career woman through and through. It was time to take a break. When Aunty Vi's estate came through and she left me the house, I decided to move up here for a while.'

'The rumour was that Rendell bought old Ma Carmichael's place as the locals call it. It was an affectionate term.'

'I remember. So you can take us out there?

'I can.'

'That would be fantastic.'

Jiminy pulled the gate to the marina shut behind him and the loud clang startled a flock of parrots in the tree above us. 'Do you remember where I used to live with Mum and Dad?'

'No, I don't know where you lived. I only ever knew you on the ferry on the way to school and when you worked on the ferry that took me out to the island.'

'We live up on the hill past *Qualia*. Next door to where I grew up.' He grinned. 'I'm afraid I've led a boring life. I've never left the islands.'

'I don't think that's boring. It's the most beautiful place in the world.'

'We're happy here. *Qualia* is a flash resort. We're about a hundred metres past it. Why don't you and your friends come up tomorrow? It's well signposted. You can meet Sara and the kids, and we'll work out the best time to go on Sunday. I'll check the tides.'

'That sounds perfect.'

'Say late afternoon tomorrow? Come for sundowners.' Jiminy stopped at the end of the road that led to a small car park where the loaded truck was parked.

'We'll see you then.'

'Good to have you home, Pippa.' Jiminy waved and headed off towards the truck.

I nodded slowly as they drove off. It was good to be back in the islands, but I wouldn't be home until we set foot on Pentecost Island the day after tomorrow.

If all went to plan, I was going to be home for a long time.

Chapter 8

Pippa

Hearing what Jiminy had to say about the new resident on the island had got me thinking. I wasn't worried about the local gossip, because no matter what was said or believed to be true, the bottom line was I was the legal owner of at least half of the island, and Aunty Vi's sprawling house on the eastern point

No. It wasn't Aunty Vi's house. It was *my* house, *my* land, and half *my* island.

And all my future.

But there was a new consideration to take into account. What happened with the island, and the house, and what I could do with it, might depend on this person who owned the other half. Wondering how I could find out more about this guy, I knew, unless I wanted to get a rehash of the gossip, I couldn't just wander around Hamilton Island asking questions.

Maybe I could ring Mr Morton at the solicitor's office?

I glanced at my watch, but it was almost five and, being Friday afternoon, I doubted whether I'd be able to get onto him. I bit my lip and stared at the whitewashed wall of the hotel as I approached. If I left the call too long, and there was no phone service on the island, I wouldn't be able to find out anything about this mystery guy who had come from nowhere to be a half owner of Aunty Vi's island.

My island.

I was still wondering what to do when I spotted Tam and Nell on the balcony of the outdoor bar.

They were each holding a fancy cocktail glass filled with a bright green frothy concoction.

'You've started early.' I climbed the steps and pulled up a stool and leaned back with a contented sigh.

'Mocktails. Pineapple and lime. We were hot after our walk,' Nell said. 'And shopping.'

Tam nudged me. 'Hep, Pip. Check out the cute barman. He was checking out Nellie here and they had a very long conversation about the one that she'd like best.'

Nell flushed beetroot red. 'Tamsin, stop it! He was only asking what my favourite fruit was.'

Tam winked at me as she kept teasing Nell. 'Trust me. He was chatting you up, girlfriend.'

'He was not.' Nell's voice was indignant, and the blush spread to her neck. When we went out, Nell was always the quiet one, and any time a guy came near her, her confidence instantly disappeared. I'd often wondered what made her that way, but she'd never shared. Tam said something had happened at uni, but Nell had never told us any more. But we had both noticed how she retreated into herself as soon as a guy showed any interest in her.

'A mocktail sounds good to me. I've had a long walk and I have news.' The barman was at my side before I could even think about a drink—he *was* cute, but not my type. In fact, after Darren, I had decided that no man was my type. I might do an Aunty Vi and live on the family island until I was old. I couldn't help grinning at the barman as I ordered my drink. 'One of those, please.'

'Certainly, madame.' With a

wide smile and an exaggerated half-bow, for God's sake, he headed back to the bar.

I loosened my shoulders and focused on relaxing. 'How did you go?'

Nell leaned forward, her face almost back to its usual colour 'Great. The general provision store has got everything we need.'

'You're exaggerating, Nell.' Tam laughed. 'It's got the basics, so don't go expecting gourmet meals straight up.'

I shook my head with a smile. 'We sure don't expect that yet. I don't even know if we'll have a stove. Or power. So long as we've got bread and cold meat, and fruit, and an esky with some ice we'll survive the first few days, so let's just see how we go. Your job is to keep us fed while we sort out a boat and communication. We're going to be working our butts off for the first few days, I think.'

'Do you know how much I'm looking forward to this?' Nell spread her hands and gestured to the lush foliage hanging above the balcony, and then out to the calm blue sea. 'No way is this going to be hard work. No traffic, no car fumes, no crowds, and just a gorgeous view to look at.'

'It's been fun wandering around the island today getting that atmosphere and thinking that we're going to create something like this. On a smaller scale, of course,' Tam added.

'It's going to take a while,' I said. 'But yes, hopefully we are. I think—I hope— we can make a go of it.'

Tam leaned back and lifted her green drink. 'Time will tell. And if it doesn't work out, well, we'll have given it our best shot.'

As I looked at my two best friends, the warm and fuzzies hit me. They were good people and had remained loyal to me through my ups and downs. Now they were going to take a chance and had moved up here to help me establish the resort that Aunty Vi had dreamed of.

How lucky was I to have picked these two women as friends all those years ago?

'After this drink, it's time for some bubbles to celebrate being here. And then I think we should go out somewhere nice for dinner to suss out the restaurants.'

Tam laughed. 'Any excuse for bubbles with you, Pippa.'

'Okay, maybe you're right, but we do have some celebrating to do. And I want you two to know how much I love you both and how grateful I am that you've come to the islands with me.'

'Such an awful place to be,' Tam said with a smile.

'Thank you.' I said as the barman put my drink on the table.

Nell looked down.

'In a few minutes could we please have a bottle of champagne and three glasses?' I asked.

'Sure. I'll be right back.' He tried to catch Nell's eye, but she wasn't having a bar of it. Tam and I exchanged a look.

'There's an Italian restaurant at the end of the street here and I sussed out the menu,' Tam said after a moment. 'It looked divine.'

'As you do.' I closed my eyes as I sipped the fruit drink. It was sweet and bitter at the same time. 'Sounds good. Do you think we should book?'

'I'll ask the barman when he

brings the bubbles. Unless you want to, Nell?'

'I am immune to your teasing, Tamsin.' Nell pulled a face. 'I'm used to it.'

The bubbles were delivered, and poured into crystal flutes, and when Nell, with a defiant glare at Tam, asked the barman about the need to book at the Italian restaurant, he offered to ring and book a table for us.

'Thank you,' Nell said quietly. When he'd gone back to the bar, she lifted her glass. 'To us. And to . . . I think we need a name for the resort, Pippa.'

I lifted my glass. 'To us. To friendship. We'll think of a name at dinner.'

'And to success,' added Tam as we clinked glasses. 'I think we should make a night of it and all get glammed up. It might be a while before we go out again.'

'Can't I go like this?' Nell didn't look impressed.

'You can't wear shorts and a T-shirt out for dinner, Nell.'

'Okay. Long pants and a T-shirt then. I didn't bring any good clothes. They're all in storage.'

Tam lifted her glass again 'Not a problem. There is a perfectly good resort wear shop opposite reception. We'll go shopping after our bubbles.'

'I agree. They won't take shorts and T-shirts at that restaurant. It looked pretty upmarket,' I added.

'All right. There might be one dress in my suitcase.' Nell pulled a face.

'Oh my God, Nell brought a dress?' Tam put her hand to her chest in mock surprise.

Nell pulled a face. 'Just as well

I'm not the sensitive type. I don't know how I'll put up with you pair on a deserted island for too long.'

'Not so deserted, apparently,' I said with a frown. 'But I'll tell you all about that over dinner.'
##

Polishing off a bottle of bubbles didn't take long with three of us, and it was only an hour later that we were all glammed up and walking along the street to the restaurant that Nell's barman had booked for us.

'You look gorgeous, Nell. You should wear dresses more often,' I said.

Nell shook her head. 'Nope, I'm happier in my shorts and tees. My red lipstick dresses me up.'

Tam and I giggled. We were all happy and talkative as we walked along, and I linked my arms with my friends. 'I haven't felt this relaxed since—'

'Since before you met the dazzling Dazza,' Tam said drily.

'Yep, I'd agree with that,' Nell said. 'It's good to have the old Pippa back.'

'Not so old,' I protested.

'We are,' Tam said. 'We'll have our big thirtieths on the island.'

I chuckled. 'And we'll probably be too tired to celebrate.'

It was early but the restaurant was already half-full as we waited at the door. The maître d' came over and greeted us.

'A table for three, *bellas*?'

'We've booked. But I'm not sure what name it was booked under, 'I said.

He ran his finger down the reservations list. 'A ha. I have found it. A booking that says three beautiful ladies." He looked at us with a smile. 'I presume that is you, unless you are being joined by more?'

'No, we are three,' I said.

He led us across the restaurant, and we were tucked into a corner alcove but beside a large window that gave us a view of the water

'I hope when you build our little restaurant—' Tam began.

'Hey, enough of this little, 'I said. 'It might be small, but it will be exclusive.'

Nell rolled her eyes. 'Did you find out how we can get over to the island, before we start making these grandiose plans?' She leaned back as the waiter picked up the linen napkin and flicked it open onto her lap.

'You won't believe it, but I came across one of my old friends who used to be a deckie on the ferry when I was at high school.

Jiminy's going to take us out to the island on Sunday, in his boat. He's invited us up to meet his family tomorrow, and to organise what we need to do.'

'Jiminy?' Tam grinned. 'As in Jiminy Cricket in the cartoons?'

'No, it wasn't cartoons,' Nell interrupted. 'It was Pinocchio. We used to watch it when we were kids. Remember, Tam?'

'Jiminy is his real name and he's a great guy,' I said. 'He used to look out for me when I started at the new school when I left Brisbane.'

The drink waiter hovered beside the table and waited for us to stop speaking. 'Here is the drinks menu, ladies. I'll go and get some water and I'll be back to take your orders for drinks in a moment.'

Deciding against another bottle

of bubbles, we each ordered a glass of wine. 'Might be more expensive, but it will save us a headache in the morning,' I said. I'd managed to let go of *most* of my worries now that I'd found a way to get to Pentecost Island, but I wanted to have a clear head.

Tam and Nell were talking about the order they were going to place at the store tomorrow and I let my thoughts roam. The anticipation of getting out to the island where I had spent my formative teen years was building.

I frowned. Damn, in the rush to get ready, I'd forgotten to Google that guy on the island. I was tempted to pull my phone out, but I resisted. When Tam and Nell drew breath, I jumped in.

'I have more news too. Apparently, we have a neighbour on the island.'

'A neighbour? I didn't know there were other houses there?' Tam said.

I shook my head. 'There didn't used to be. Jiminy said this guy's built a house at the other end of the bay and is a bit of a recluse.'

'Will it affect your plans to open a resort?' asked the ever-sensible Nell.

I shrugged. 'I guess that's what we have to find out. Actually, that's part of your brief, Nell. If you don't mind. If you're happy to, I'd be really pleased if you could chase up permits and all that sort of stuff. I wouldn't have a clue where to start. I've been thinking about all of our strengths and what we need to assign to each of us.'

Tam put her hand up with a giggle. 'I bags cooking.'

'That's a given. But I guess until we get out there, we don't know what we'll have to do first up.'

'I was joking. You know I'll help with anything that needs doing. I won't be cooking for a good while. Let's just focus on relaxing tonight,' Tam said. 'Once we get to the island, we'll be able to divvy up our responsibilities.'

We all agreed and an hour later—and another glass of wine each— our giggles were louder and more frequent as we talked about our plans.

'Maybe we could hold celebrity weddings on the island,' Tam said.

'Maybe we could offer it for that Survivor TV show,' Nell added. She'd relaxed and managed a pretty smile for the waiter as he brought our bowls of chilli crab linguini to the table.

I let out a satisfied sigh and sat back as Tam dissected her meal and tried to work out the recipe.

'Definitely one for our restaurant,' Nell said as she wiped the sauce from her plate with a piece of garlic bread. 'And come on, you gals, we have to think of a name for the resort and the restaurant too.'

I nodded, but my attention wandered when my gaze settled on the couple sitting at the table across from us. They were having an intense conversation and their voices carried across to me as there was a lull in the background music. The woman's back was to me, and her white-blonde hair was done up in an elegant French roll held by a diamond clip.

I could tell a real diamond at thirty paces.

Jewellery was my weakness, but one that Darren had never picked up on, even with many hints from me over the time we were together. The woman sat stiffly, and her shoulders were so straight and still, the tension between them almost twanged in the air.

I let my gaze move to the guy across from her, and my breath caught.

My God. What a beautiful face. Even with the frown that marred his forehead. He was so good-looking he could have been a movie star. My mouth dried as I stared at him. Jet-black hair hung over eyes set wide above chiselled cheekbones. His olive skin had twin patches of pink high on his cheeks, and full lips and a five o'clock shadow gave him a rakish look. When he lifted his head to look at his partner, his eyes were a brilliant blue.

I had never seen such a gorgeous face in real life. On the

movie screen maybe, but not in the flesh. It was hard to look away, but as he wasn't looking in my direction, I kept watching. His attention was totally focused on the woman across from him.

He was gorgeous maybe, but definitely not happy by the set of those lips.

I felt like a voyeur as his gaze flicked over to meet mine. He must have sensed my interest. I was stunned by the intensity of his stare and I couldn't look away. His eyes were almost challenging me.

To do what? Look embarrassed? Look away?

I did neither and simply let my eyes hold his. The strange feeling in the pit of my stomach was one I had never felt before.

Finally, he broke that connection as he turned back to the woman. I felt sorry for her.

They were obviously having an argument about something, and I felt as though I had intruded on a private moment. An angry moment.

How sad to come to a beautiful place like this for a holiday and be unhappy.

I shrugged and turned my attention back to my friends.

'The Happy Life Island Resort,' I said.

Tam and Nell stared at me and both shook their heads.

'Ugh, yuk. No.' Tam pretended to put a finger down her throat.

I smiled and tried not to look back at the guy across from me. 'Okay. Hit me with some names.'

Chapter 9
Rafe

I forced my eyes away from the woman who'd held my gaze.

Jenny reached out and took my hand and her eyes were hard. 'Rafe, it's been two years and you haven't taken on board what we said. You have to listen, and you have to get over what happened.'

'Get over it?' The words burst from my mouth just as there was a lull in the conversations in the noisy restaurant and a few heads turned.

'With the advance you've accepted you're going to have to give us something,' she said. 'Something without the cynical viewpoint, and such stereotypical females.'

'Straight to the point, I see. A phone call would have done it.' I stared at her. 'Jenny, if that's the only reason you came all this way, you've had a wasted trip. You can go back to London and tell Bryant I don't give a flying fu . . .fig if it takes me twenty years to write this book. If that doesn't suit, I'll give you the advance back. I'm not ready yet. How many times do I have to tell you that?' I was angry—as I was too often these days—but I kept my voice low. 'I don't even know that I can deliver what you want anymore.'

The candle in the middle of the table flickered as a gust of wind blew in from the water. As the restaurant had filled, the waiter had opened a concertina glass door, and we now had an uninterrupted view of the water and the setting sun. The colour of the sky was beautiful, but I didn't care. Once I would have been storing words in my head or pulling out the notebook I had always carried with me.

Jenny's fingers tightened on my wrist. 'We don't want the advance back. You must write this book. If you don't, it is a criminal waste of your talent.'

My laugh was cynical. 'A waste of my talent? Or a waste of the money that Little Hampton would make when they publish it? Don't talk shit to me, Jenny. I've always had an honest relationship with you and Bryant, so don't let me down now.'

She held my gaze, but her gaze wavered a fraction. She'd been sent to do a job, and I knew Bryant had hoped that I would give in because I cared about Jenny. Jenny and Bryant knew me too well. They were the owners of Little Hampton Publishing—which had published my first three books and we had become friends over the past five years.

I knew I could make a life without another book. I was making a lot of adjustments lately—for the past seven hundred and one days if I was counting—and I didn't need any more pressure on me, so I took refuge in sarcasm.

'Really, Jenny? You tell me it will be a loss to the world? A criminal waste, you say?' I laughed. 'How sad that you and Bryant won't make all that lovely money if I don't write it. Isn't it all about having another bestseller? Isn't that what publishing is all about? You take my creative work and you turn it into a book. You give it an enticing cover, check I haven't made any mistakes and then you send it out to the world.

You want me to follow it around from town to town, to country to country, and then you guys make ten times the money I do.'

My sigh was long and low when Jenny's eyes glinted with tears in the flickering candlelight.

'I know you don't mean any of that. I can see through you, Rafe. It's a cover for how you're feeling. If it makes you feel better to lash out at me, go ahead. I can take it. I just want you to stop beating *yourself* up. *It. Wasn't. Your. Fault.*'

A glimmer of regret spiked though me and I pulled my hand away. I looked down at the red and white checked tablecloth. 'I'm sorry Jenny. I know I'm being a proper bastard but that's the way I am these days. I'm better off away from people, and then I can't lash out.'

Her voice was soft. 'You haven't always been this way, Rafe. I know you've buried yourself away on this tropical island. How much longer are you going to cut yourself off from civilisation? When are you coming home?'

'I am home, Jen.' I reached out and took her hand again and tried to soften my words with a gentle touch. 'And this is all the civilisation I want. This is where I'm going to stay.'

'Rafe, please. You have to listen to me. You know we love you like one of our family. It's not the publication we're worried about. Alright, it is a small part of it,' she conceded. 'But we worry about *you*. On this island by yourself. What if you had an accident? Who do you talk to each day? Who would even know if you needed help?'

'No one, and quite frankly, Jenny, it suits me like that.'

'That makes me sad.'

'You think *you* know sad?' My words tumbled out and I couldn't hold them back. 'You try it for a while. See what it's like to lose the person you loved. It's destroyed my faith, and with that, my ability to trust. And if that's impacting on my writing, I'm sorry, that's the way it is.' My voice was harsh. 'I don't want to get over it. It was a very good lesson in life.'

'I think you're doing yourself a disservice, Rafe. Do you think you need professional help to work through these feelings?'

My laugh was bitter. 'So I can write this next blockbuster for you guys?'

'What are you trying to achieve living over here? What do you do with your day?' Jenny's voice trembled. 'I'm going to be hard on you here.'

'Okay, hit me with it.'

'Just remember we love you. We *do*. I thought we had a friendship. What we don't want is to see you wallowing in self-pity for the rest of your life. As hard as it is to say, Rafe, you were let down by Rebecca. It happens every day to lots of people, but you've taken it too personally. Burying yourself away over here has just built the hurt up in your eyes, and, when you analyse it, was it really that bad?'

'So you're a psychologist, now too, Jenny?'

'Maybe. Please promise me that you'll think about it? Forget the book, but please, please try to get over it. Seek some help. Talk to someone.'

I dropped my gaze to the

table. I couldn't stand that look in her eyes. It made me feel like a right bastard. 'I know you both just want the right thing for me, but Jen, I'm not ready to write. I'm sorry, I don't know how I'm ever going to be ready again.'

She opened her mouth to answer, but the waiter interrupted before she could speak. Neither of us had noticed him standing there and he looked embarrassed as he handed us each a menu. 'I'll give you a few minutes to decide.' He gestured to a board that was propped against the empty table beside us. 'They are the specials of the day. I can highly recommend the crab. It is caught fresh each day.'

In one of my books I'd questioned the meaningless things that make up each day of our life. What did it matter what we ate?

What music we listened to? Where we went? I must have had a premonition. One that my life ahead was going to be this vacuum that I had lived in for the past two years.

As much as I hated to admit it to myself—or Jenny—her words had touched me. I knew I was a selfish bastard, but I told myself if I lived my life in isolation, I wouldn't impact on anyone else.

'It's called depression, Rafe,' she said quietly.

As we sat there in silence a peal of laughter caught my attention. The woman who had looked at me before was sitting with two others I hadn't noticed previously. As always, I took note of what was around me; it was a habit I'd had all of my life. I'd been interested in people and that was what had driven my storytelling once.

The woman who'd held my gaze was stunning; her hair was the colour of a pale apricot, her skin was flawless, her eyes beautiful, but her eyes held an empty sadness that I recognised. The other two women were laughing as they spoke; the one with short dark hair had expressive hands that she used nonstop with gestures that accompanied her words, and the other—a well-endowed blonde with messy curls sat back and watched, but the woman I focused on laughed as she listened to them. The three women were all dressed in bright colours, and they filled the restaurant with vibrancy and life.

Even the one with the sad eyes.

What would it feel like to be happy again? To have the joy of life within, and when there was nothing more important than sharing a meal and happy times with friends? For the first time in a long time, interest rippled through me and I wondered what they were laughing about.

At the ripe age of thirty-five I had turned into a bitter man. I knew I needed to pull myself out of this morass of pity I lived in every day and I knew that if I was to survive emotionally, I was going to have to make some changes in my life.

I jumped when Jenny spoke. I must have voiced my thoughts aloud.

'Yes, Rafe. That's what you have to do. Why don't you come back to the UK with me? Bryant found this really good retreat in the Cotswolds. I'm sure it would help you.'

'A rehab centre for the terminally pissed off? Maybe I could write a book about that while I was there?'

I felt bad when Jenny's eyes welled with tears again.

'I'm sorry, that was my version of a joke.'

She didn't reply.

'All right. I'll try to get something to you in the next few months. Is that enough of a promise?'

'That's a start. If we haven't got anything from you by the end of the year, we'll have to reconsider the contract. If it was just Bryant and I, it wouldn't matter, but we have shareholders that we have to answer to, Rafe.'

'I understand totally,' I said in my business voice.

We sat in silence until the water came back to take our order.

The laughter from the table near the window was infectious. One of the women had a giggle that made me want to smile. I saw Jenny glance over at them.

'Good to see happy people having a good time,' I said to lighten the atmosphere.

She nodded.

The waiter returned and placed a bowl of bread sticks on the table.

'Are you ready to order?' His pen was poised over the notepad.

Jenny looked at me and I shrugged.

'We'll both have the crab you recommended.' She passed the menus to him.

When he'd gone Jenny looked at me. 'You've lost a lot of weight, Rafe.'

'I don't need to eat much. I expend very little energy sitting at a desk looking at a blank screen all day.'

The heavy silence descended again. As we sat there the woman with the apricot hair rose and walked across the restaurant past our table. Her eyes were downcast, and I got the impression she was trying to avoid making eye contact.

My gaze stayed on her back as she passed the table. Her hair hung to her waist like a rippling fall of water. She turned her head as one of the other women called out to her.

'Pippa! Ask for the dessert menu on your way back.'

Pippa. The name suited her. If I'd been creating a character with that name, she would have looked exactly like the woman now standing at the bar. As I stared our eyes connected. She lifted her chin and didn't look away until the barman came to take her order.

For a moment, I frowned; I'd heard that name before, but I couldn't remember where.

But for some unknown reason, I had felt myself come alive a fraction, and it hurt like hell.

Chapter 10

Pippa

I always woke up with the sun, and on Sunday morning, I was packed and ready to go two hours before we were due to meet Jiminy at the marina. Tam, Nell and I each had a suitcase and a backpack—Jiminy had organised to have our provisions delivered straight to the marina at nine o'clock this morning—so there was little to take down with us apart from our luggage.

The afternoon before had been pleasant. Jiminy's wife, Sara, was shy, but their two children had made up for her quietness, talking nineteen to the dozen and wanting to know all about the island we were going to live on.

'Will there be pirates?' Baden had asked. 'And buried treasure?'

'Can we come and visit?' his sister interrupted.

'It would be way cool to have visitors,' I'd said. 'You make sure you get your dad to bring you out to see us.'

Baden had a lunchtime birthday party to attend today so Jiminy was running us out by himself, and then heading straight back to Hamo.

Their house was set high on a hill and looked out over the Whitsunday Passage. I'd never get tired of looking at the incredible blue water, no matter how long I lived there.

Seeing Jiminy and his tightknit little family had made me a little bit sad, and this morning that emotion was mixed with the anticipation of going out to the island. It was times like that when I felt lonely and knowing that I had no family—unless you counted Aunty Vi's sons, my two distant second cousins in England—always had me searching for someone to love.

No more, I chastised myself sternly. Remember Darren.

I glanced at my phone. It wasn't even seven yet, and I was showered and packed. I unzipped my suitcase and pulled out my joggers and a pair of socks. I'd go for a walk and be back in time to have breakfast with Tam and Nell before we went down to meet Jiminy at the marina.

I pulled my hair into a high ponytail, slipped my socks and joggers on, and then closed the door of the hut behind me. There was no sign of life from the two other huts where Tam and Nell were sleeping. I set off for the hill that led up from Whitsunday

Boulevard to a lookout called One Tree Hill. I breathed deeply as I walked and the slight unhappiness that had dogged me all night was soon replaced with serenity. I strode up the hill and was puffing with exertion by the time I reached the lookout, but the effort had been worth it. A spreading poinciana tree, massed with brilliant red flowers, caught my breath. The lush green grass was covered with petals and the bench seat in the middle of the lawn beckoned, but I straightened and looked across the water. A series of bays indented the shore of the island.

This lookout faced to the north, so I couldn't see the volcanic peak of *my* island rising from the sea to the south east. As I stood there drinking in the vista below me, footsteps broke the silence as another early morning jogger took on the challenge of One Tree Hill.

I made my way to the edge of the small cleared area and turned away from the road. I wasn't in the mood for talking to anyone. I wanted to appreciate this view and get my thoughts in order.

I waited until the footsteps had faded again and I turned around to head back down to the resort. To my surprise, someone was sitting on the bench seat beneath the tree and I put my head down as I walked past.

'Good morning.' The voice was deep and held a cultured English accent.

I lifted my head, prepared to nod and keep walking, but was taken aback to see the same man who'd locked eyes with me last night in the Italian restaurant.

My steps slowed as he looked

at me, and again I felt that strange pull into his eyes.

'Good morning,' I replied as heat filled my face.

I put my head down, and hurried towards the road down the hill, relieved when he didn't speak again.

Despite the walk back being downhill, my heart was still pounding hard when I reached the resort and went back to my beachside hut. I was still hot, so after I took my shoes and socks off and put my canvas sneakers on, I washed my face with cool water. I stared at myself in the mirror, wondering why one person and such a brief encounter could have had such an impact on me.

It must be because he was such a fine-looking man.
##
I met Tam and Nell in the

breakfast room of the resort. On the way I checked out of my hut, leaving my suitcase and backpack at reception. The girls were buzzing with excitement. Keeping in the nautical mood, Tam had shed her usual dress and was wearing a pair of 1940s high waisted shorts and a *pink* T-shirt patterned with white sailing boats. Her curls were held back by a pink bandana. She looked gorgeous but . . .

'Did you have to wear pink today, Tamsin?' I said.

'A new start for all of us, Pip dear.' she said with her arms folded. 'You—we—are leaving the past behind us. I found the T-shirt at one of the stores in the shopping street and I couldn't resist. It's loose enough not to cling to any wobbly bits.'

'Oh, for goodness sake,' I said

crossly, forgetting about the pink. 'You look great. I'll forget about pink if you accept that you are *not* fat.'

Tam bobbed her head and the two high pigtails jiggled and she looked about eighteen. 'All right, I will. And pink will be fine anyway.'

'Hope so,' I muttered as I picked up the coffee pot and poured a straight black before I sat down.

'Excited, Pippa?' Nell was dressed in her usual khaki shorts and T-shirt.

'A bit. I couldn't sleep,' I replied after the first slug of coffee hit my bloodstream. 'I was up at the crack of dawn and went for a walk. To be honest, I've been worrying about what we're going to find there.'

'Better to be realistic, and not be disappointed,' Tam said.

Nell stood and went over to the breakfast bar and came back with a plate loaded with fresh fruit. 'For sharing.'

'Thanks, Nellie,' I said.

'Have I got time to have a hot brekky?' Tam asked. 'The menu looks interesting, and I want to see how they present it.'

I pulled out my phone and checked the time. 'We have thirty-five minutes to eat and get to the marina, so you'll have to be quick.'

'We'll need the energy.' Tam jumped up and went over to the waitress to place her order.

I picked up a small piece of watermelon and nibbled on it. 'I don't think I can eat anything much.'

'You okay, sweets?' Nell asked. 'You look a bit pale on it.'

'Yeah. Just nervous. I wonder if I've made a huge mistake. Maybe I should have stayed away and just put Aunty Vi's house on the market. If this doesn't work out, it's going to be twice as hard to leave the island again.'

Nell shook her head. 'What happened to the two Ps? Positivity, Pip!'

I chuckled. 'I guess Darren and losing my job happened. You're right, Nell. I've been in a strange mood since dinner last night. I need to pull myself up. It will be fine, and if it's not, we'll make sure it is.'

'That's better.' Nell nodded and smiled.

Twenty minutes later, Tam had demolished the strangest looking— green—eggs I had ever seen— and Nell and I had cleared the fruit plate. I stood and gestured to the door.

'Come on you pair, the first

day of the rest of our lives is about to begin.' I giggled. 'Tam, you've got egg yolk all the way down the front of your fancy pink T-shirt. You'll have to get changed, love.'

I couldn't help my smirk.

'Can't take you anywhere.' Nell nudged Tam and giggled with me.

'I'll go and sponge it in the ladies.' Tam flounced off and Nell's infectious giggle had me smiling.

Tam was quick, and we loaded our bags into one of the electric buggies at reception and were down at the marina in no time.

'Hey, Pippa! Over here.' Jiminy called from a boat halfway along the first wharf, and we wheeled our suitcases down the ramp, and along the wharf. Even though it was coming into winter, the sun was warm. The water glistened as the seabirds swooped overhead. My mood kept improving with each step I took.

'Morning, gals. It's a great day to be on the water.'

'Nice boat, Jim,' I said.

'She is, and even better, she's all mine.'

An engine roared on the other side of the wharf and a huge black speedboat took off into the channel leaving a wake of white foam behind.

'But a man can dream,' Jiminy said gesturing towards the black boat that was quickly disappearing. 'One day I might have something like that. If I win Lotto, that is.'

I gestured to the rows of luxury boats opposite where his boat was berthed. 'There seems to be more expensive boats here than when I caught the ferry to school.'

He nodded. 'There's a lot on international boaties make the marina their home base, and they sail and motor around the islands in the winter.'

'Did you hear that, Tam? If we could set up some sort of mooring, there's an instant clientele for the restaurant.'

'Big plans, Pippa?' Jiminy said.

We hadn't gone into much detail when we'd visited his place yesterday.

'Some plans, but we have to suss out the island first. It's a while since I've been there.'

'Be prepared,' he said. 'Years of tropical growth, a cyclone and a couple of big blows might have done some damage to the old house.'

'Only one way to find out. Are we ready to go?'

'Yep. Your provisions were delivered half an hour ago, and they're stored below.'

'Thank you.' I turned to Jiminy.

'Let's go!'

The deck vibrated beneath my feet as he started the motors. I found a spot near the helm and stared ahead, waiting for that first magnificent view of Pentecost Island to appear as we rounded the point. Centuries of volcanic debris had fused into solid rock, and the way that my island—*yes, my island*—rose from the depths of the Coral Sea was nothing short of spectacular. The first time I had seen it as a lonely eleven-year-old had made a tremendous impression that had stayed with me over the years.

Magical was the word I'd used back in those early days with Aunty Vi.

It had been magical. I had healed on that island, and I had learned to be strong and independent.

It was time to do it again.

Jiminy steered us out into the passage and headed south, following in the wake of the black boat. He put his hands to his eyes as he looked ahead. 'I thought it might have been.'

'Might have been what?' I asked.

'Your neighbour on the island. He has a boat like that, but it's unusual to see him out and about. You never know, you might be lucky enough to meet him on your first day.'

I shook my head. 'No, my first day is going to be spent having a look at the place. Is there phone service this far out, Jim?'

'Yes, there's service all the way down to the Shaw group of islands these days.' He turned the boat in a wide arc to miss the rocky peninsula as we neared the southern point of Hamilton Island.

'There she is,' I exclaimed excitedly as my impressive island came into view. She rose almost two hundred metres above the sea at her highest point and it wasn't until you got close that you could see the wide and flat parts of the island around the base of the mountain. Aunty Vi's house was tucked into the side of the hill overlooking a bay on the north side of the volcanic peak. According to Jiminy, the new neighbour's house would be far away enough not to bother us. At a pinch we might see his lights at night, but I could live with that.

I just hoped that he could too.

The information that he was a recluse didn't reassure me. I wondered how he'd feel about a resort development on the island.

Anyway, we'd been here first.

The house and island had been in the Carmichael family since the 1930s, when the islands had first been settled. Hopefully he wouldn't spend a lot of time here if he was some rich dude.

I leaned back with a contented sigh as Jiminy turned the boat towards Pentecost Island.

I was on my way home.

Chapter 11

Rafe

Jenny's flight to Cairns, the first leg of her flight home, left early and I'd made a quick trip to the general provisions store on the island. I placed a large order of meat, fresh fruit and vegetables and arranged to have them delivered to my boat immediately. The pantry in the house had enough dry goods to see me out a few more months. It cost me an extra fifty dollars on top of what I'd paid for the groceries to get it down there straight away, but it was worth every cent. I was anxious to get back to my island.

On the way to the marina, I called into the bottle shop and picked up a bottle of Glenfiddich whisky. I resisted the temptation to get half a dozen. I'd made Jenny a promise that I would start work and taking comfort in no more than two whiskies each night would help me keep my promise.

Somehow talking with Jenny had opened something in me. When I woke up in the hotel room this morning the heavy feeling that pressed on my chest as soon as I became aware each day had lightened a little. I'm not sure where it came from, but I embraced that unfamiliar lightness.

Jenny had hugged me tight as I'd waited in the departure hall with her.

'You take care of yourself, Rafe. Bryant and I worry about you all the time. You are a dear friend, you know'—she held my gaze intently—'and we worry about you.'

I nodded tersely and quickly returned her hug and stepped back. I was a typical Englishman and I showed little emotion to the world. Maybe that was half of the problem as to why I was having trouble moving on with life.

As I stood in my boat heading towards my island refuge an hour later, I realised that I felt better than I had for a long time.

It was a brilliant June day and I drew in a deep breath and filled my lungs with clean, salt-laden air. The manor house in the Cotswolds she had suggested for "recovery" was not one bit tempting, despite the wonderful location and cooler weather. For the first time, a smile tugged at my lips. I would seek my own healing here.

Jenny and Bryant were good friends; they were probably the only people in the world who knew where to find me and the only ones who cared.

I had no other friends left and

I had no wife.

I took a deep breath and inhaled the salty air to banish the anger that came knocking with that thought.

'I am in paradise,' I said beneath my breath. 'I own a beautiful house on a tropical island. Money is not a problem and I have a book to finish. I promised Jenny and I'll do my best to get something done.' Saying the words aloud made them real.

Maybe I should talk to myself more.

I glanced behind and eased back on the throttle as I approached Pentecost Island. When I'd seen the portion of the island advertised for sale, the name of the island had caught my attention.

I had flown down from Cairns to see the property, and the island had instantly hooked me. I'd wanted to isolate myself, and here was the perfect place to build the house I had always wanted. I made an offer to Vi Carmichael the same day. I had offered her triple what she was asking so I could buy the whole island, but she refused.

'Half or nothing. No point trying to make me budge, boy, because I won't.'

She'd been an interesting woman, and once I accepted her terms, we'd sealed it with a handshake and a whisky. The plans for the house were already in my head, so I had them drawn up, signed a builder and the house was finished within four months. Amazing how money talked.

I'd known—or hoped— that I could be happy in a beautiful setting like this.

The island is dramatic in the

way it rises from the sea. Cloaked in forests of eucalypts and pine, with shadowy gullies of rainforest as you climb around the mountain, there are many places you can walk. Rocky granite outcrops amongst the forest add to the desolate geology of the island. On each end of the island is a swathe of verdant green grass. My home sat above one such clearing, and the other grassy flat is near the old abandoned house on the north end of my bay.

As I turned, I spotted two sailing catamarans heading south towards Shaw Island. Behind them was a motor launch, and as I watched, it turned to the portside, and headed towards the island.

Since the cyclone that had hit the region in the first month after my arrival, the bay on the north-western side was impassable.

There was only one entry into the bay on the eastern side beneath my house on the cliff now, and to my knowledge it was not widely known. I had watched a few catamarans come to grief at low tide on the exposed reef where the previous entrance to the channel on the northern point had once let boats enter. Ma Carmichael had told me that over the years it had been a popular place for an overnight mooring, and she had called it Happy Bay.

'I made lots of friends from all over the world on those years,' she'd told me one night as we sat on my veranda overlooking the mooring. 'But when my niece came to live with me, I didn't think it was the right thing to do. Partying down on the sand each night with folk who were looking for good times in happy company. Over the years when Pippa was here, fewer boats came to moor in my bay each winter.' She'd lifted the tumbler to her lips and sighed. 'When Pippa left for university, I figured I was too old for that party scene any more.'

Pippa! I knew I'd heard that name before when the woman in the restaurant had called out last night.

Surely that beautiful woman wasn't the same Pippa that Ma had talked about? It would be too much of a coincidence.

As I eased my craft through the passage between the coral heads, I stared at the launch that was stopped at the outer edge of the bay. The skipper was pointing across the bay to where the old house was hidden behind the forest. I cut the engine and I waited and watched. The old house at that end was a solid structure and had survived the recent cyclone. It had been empty since Ma had left and the only life there now was the wild goats I occasionally saw. The last time I had walked over there, the trees had grown over the house like a canopy, increasingly encroaching on the dwelling.

A couple of times the skipper ventured close to the reef, but he obviously knew what he was doing because he pulled up each time he came close to the coral that would be exposed at low tide.

To my dismay on his third attempt he somehow crossed the coral and the boat made its way to the shore.

What the hell did he think he was doing?

There were others on the boat with him and I stared, waiting to see what they were going to do. Technically they had every right to be there as my property boundary extended only halfway along the bay, but on the few occasions that boats had managed to moor at my end of the island over the past months, they'd listened to me and had soon left when I told them it was private land. I watched as he climbed over and untied the rope of the tender and motored into the shore. He tied the rope around a lone palm tree on the beach and then got back into the tender and headed back to the launch. As I watched a woman on board passed him two white boxes. The same ones that the provisions came in from the general store.

This wasn't looking good.

Once he'd put them down a second woman passed him a couple of crates, and then a third woman appeared and passed some more boxes over.

Once they were loaded, he pulled the rope above the tender that was now secured to the launch, and that way he was able to pull the boat right up on to the beach. He unloaded the boxes and crates and then pulled his way back to the launch.

Bloody hell.

This time there were suitcases, swags and backpacks offloaded.

What did they think they were doing?

I started the motor and eased into the small wharf that I had built at the base of the cliff. I quickly unloaded my provisions, placed the bottle of whisky into my backpack and carried them up the steep path to the house.

When I reached the top, I turned around. The sound of the

launch starting drifted up to me.

The vessel was leaving the bay and, to my dismay, there were three women standing waving to the skipper. My stomach sank as I recognised them.

It *was* Ma Carmichael's Pippa.

##

Pippa

Jiminy was full of apologies that he didn't have time to come to the house with us.

'I've only got another half hour to get Baden to Daydream Island,' he said apologetically. 'Who'd ever have thought that a kids' party would be held at a resort!'

'It's fine,' I said. 'I really appreciate you bringing us over today. I wish you'd let me pay you for your time.'

He shook his head emphatically. 'A favour for a friend, Pippa. I just wish I had time to help you up to the house, and more important, check it's habitable.'

I waved my hand dismissively. 'It will be fine. Now that I know there's phone service out here'— Tam had kept a check on it the whole boat trip across— 'I'll give you a call in a day or so.'

'And if there's any problem settling in today, you call me this afternoon. Okay?'

'I promise. Now go. You don't want to be late getting your son to the party!'

Jiminy turned back to the boat and paused. 'Ah, I forgot. Did you think of buying diesel for the generator?'

'Um no.' I shook my head.

He pulled himself along to the boat and disappeared below deck. A moment later he reappeared holding up a plastic fuel container.

'Take this. I doubt there will be any at the house. This should keep you going for a few days.'

'Thank you. That was the one thing I didn't even consider. I'll pay you for that.'

'Next time.' Jiminy flashed a grin and next minute the boat was pulling away between the coral heads.

When the shingly sand on the beach crunched beneath my bare feet, I knew I was home. All my doubts faded, and happiness filled me. Although a little bit of sadness tugged, knowing that Aunty Vi wasn't up in the house waiting for me, but in the time that had passed since her death I had adjusted. At least she'd not spent a long time in the aged care home. Even though she'd tried to tell me she enjoyed living there, I'd heard the sadness in her voice when she'd talked about the island. But being away from here, it had been easy to forget and cope with grieving. This was where she had lived for most of her life. Aunty Vi had been a caring woman and she had taught me so much when I'd turned up on her doorstep. She'd taught me to believe in myself, and she taught me to trust myself. I was angry that I'd let Darren— and Eric in his own way—take that away from me over the past couple of years.

'Promise you'll go back there, one day, Pippa,' she'd said the last time I'd spoken to her.

'I promise.' But never had I imagined it would be so soon.

I was here now, and life was going to be good. I had a goal, and I knew Aunty Vi would have approved.

'How about we call it Aunty Vi's

place?' I turned to see Tam and Nell watching me. I looked around and then down at the suitcases and boxes.

Tam shook her head. 'And you call yourself a marketer? Doesn't appeal to me. No one would know who Aunty Vi was.'

Nell pointed to the boxes. 'We'd better get the food out of the sun.'

'How about we just carry everything up and put it under the trees there in the shade? It's not too hot yet, and then we'll go and check out the house.' Tam's smile was as wide as mine.

It took three trips to carry our luggage and the boxes from where Jiminy had placed them near the edge of the water up to the shade at the edge of the forest.

'Do you remember how to get to the house?' Tam asked quietly.

'Of course, I do. I lived here for eight years, remember? I was almost nineteen when I left.'

'That's over ten years ago,' Nell said.

'What's with the age thing? Please stop reminding us that we are heading for thirty.'

'Well, thirty doesn't bother me,' said Tam. 'I'll wear it like a badge of honour.'

'I'll remember that and give you a big three O badge next May,' I joked as I turned towards the gap in the trees where the path to the house began. I stood where the butterflies used to come out of the dark forest, and when I saw the path my pace quickened, as anticipation kicked in.

Home.

I could hear Tam and Nell behind me as my feet took me towards the house. They seemed to know where to go without any conscious thought. Although the path was overgrown, it was still easy to see where it had led for almost a hundred years.

Tree branches met in a beautiful lacy green arch above my head and I just had to keep an eye out for the occasional log that had fallen across the path. When I came to the small clearing where the path intersected with the track that led up to the mountain, both paths were blocked with fallen trees. It didn't bode well for the site of the house. I'd heard that it had been a ripper of a cyclone that had pummelled the islands for almost thirty-six hours. I stood with my hands on my hips and looked around for the best way to get through. On the mountain side there was a narrow gap between the fallen trees.

'Are there snakes on the island?" Nell's voice was hesitant as she caught me up. 'Will there be any under those dead trees?'

'No snakes, just death adders.'

'What!'

'And just some tree snakes and the odd brown snake and. They won't hurt you unless you stand on one.'

'Gee thanks, Pip. You've filled me with confidence.'

'It's okay. I never saw one snake the whole time I lived here.'

Tam caught up, and Nell stayed close as we squeezed through the narrow gap on the right of the fallen trees. Lizards and unseen creatures scuttled in the forest on either side and birds sang above us. It was almost as though they were greeting me.

The house was only a couple of hundred metres from the shore, but it was well hidden, tucked into the side of a small hill that protected it from the prevailing winds. Until you reached the grassy glade where the house was, you never would have guessed there was a building in the forest.

I pushed aside the foliage of the large broad-leaved bottle tree that had been there for many years. I'd spent a lot of time up that tree pretending I was in the Enid Blyton Magic Faraway tree when I was a child.

The book had probably been too young for the twelve-year-old I had been, but Aunty Vi had introduced me to fantasy books. I would climb that tree when I felt sad. As the years had passed, the memory of my Mum and Dad had faded and the time that I spent up there lessened.

I stepped into the glade and

drew a deep breath.

Taking a step towards the house I jumped as a bird squawked and flew off protesting as his peace was disturbed. Tam and Nell stepped out of the forest behind me.

'Oh wow, it looks the same as I remember,' Nell exclaimed.

Apart from the encroaching vegetation, the house itself didn't look any different, and I bit my lip as my heart filled with emotion. Aunty Vi wouldn't be stepping out to greet me like she always had when I came home from school. A couple of fallen trees blocked the path and I stepped around them and walked slowly across to the steps.

'I'd forgotten what a big house it was,' Tam said. 'I guess I thought it seemed big because I was a kid that time I came to visit you, but it is huge. Look at the verandah. It goes all the way around.'

'And look at those trees. I remember when we came to visit, you took us up a hill and made us climb a tree behind you so we could see all the islands from the top,' Nell said. 'I remember how scared I was.'

'And your Aunty Vi told us how, whenever she couldn't find you, you were guaranteed to be up a tree somewhere.'

'It wasn't that often,' I protested reaching out and touching the hand rail. It was in good condition—surprisingly all the outside timber seemed to be. I put my head back and looked up. The roof looked okay too; I couldn't see anything loose or broken. How had it escaped the ferocity of that cyclone?

'Do you have a key?' Tam asked.

I patted the small bag that was on my hip. 'I do. Mr Morton gave it to me when I went to Mackay.' I grinned. 'Just as well Darren was gone before I heard about my inheritance.'

Tam nodded. 'The smartest thing you ever did was chuck him out, otherwise he might have been here with you today and not us.'

'Maybe,' I said as I climbed the steps, the key clenched in my hand.

I'd been so focused on my own issues I hadn't thought to ask the solicitor what was at the house. I knew so little about what Aunty Vi had done when she left.

Guilt lay heavily on me, and I lifted my chin as I stepped onto the verandah. It was covered with leaves and animal droppings and the furniture that had once been here was gone.

I wondered whether it had been taken away or whether it had blown away in the cyclone. Aunty Vi had been on the mainland by then, and I'd called to check she was okay.

God, I'd been slack. It was as though I had totally shut out memories of my life up here.

And my life before I'd moved north to live with Aunty Vi.

Even when I'd talked to the therapist I'd seen for a few months after Aunty Vi had died, I hadn't ever mentioned that her death was the catalyst for my mood swings.

The front door was closed and locked and the curtains were closed at the windows that faced the verandah.

A cloud passed over the sun and a shiver ran down my back.

The air was still and quiet as though the natural world was holding its breath like I was. I jumped as Tam and Nell came up close behind me.

'Come on, Pip. Let's get inside. We need to check it out and get the food up here to the house.'

I turned around. 'Now that we know the house is intact, do you want to go and start bringing it here while I check out the inside.' I needed to be alone, but that wasn't going to happen.

Tam shook her head. 'No way. We want to see it too.'

'Okay.' I put the key in the lock and turned it. In all the time I'd lived here, the door was never closed, let alone locked.

The heavy wooden door opened with a creak. Tam and Nell were close behind me as I stepped inside. There was a small room inside the front entry, where I'd left my shoes, school bag and raincoat when I'd come off the boat every Friday.

The room was empty. No hats or rain gear hanging on the large hooks. I pushed open the door that led into the lounge room.

My eyes widened as they adjusted to the dim interior. The room was bare. A fine layer of dust covered the floorboards, but that's all that was in the room. Faded squares on the cream painted walls were all that remained of the paintings that had once hung there.

I walked across the room slowly and my sandals made little noise on the dusty floor. 'This goes through to the kitchen,' I said. 'Brace yourselves, ladies. This is going to let us know how much we're going to have to rough it for a while.'

I breathed a sigh of relief as I walked into the kitchen. The scrubbed pine table and the eight chairs were still in the middle of the old-fashioned kitchen, and a variety of pots and pans hung over the gas stove that was set back into an alcove.

'Hmmm. I didn't think of gas either, 'I said. 'I've gone soft. Too used to electric light switches and microwaves at my fingertips.'

Tam walked past me and opened some of the cupboards. 'There's still dishes and things in here, but they're going to need a good wash.'

Nell crossed to the sink and turned the tap on. There was a grinding noise and then a splutter as brown-stained water spat out of the tap into the sink. She let it run and it gradually cleared. 'We have water,' she said triumphantly. 'Come on Tam, we'll go back and start bringing the gear back. Pip, while you look around see if you can find a broom and I'll sweep through the kitchen before we put everything in here until we get sorted.'

'Thank you. I really appreciate you both being here with me. I'll check out the rest of the house and then I'll come and help.'

I was getting used to being here, and Aunty Vi's absence wasn't hurting as much. Tam and Nell headed back outside, and I walked up the hallway that led to the bedrooms, and to the large room at the back that Aunty Vi had called her studio. She'd dabbled in painting when I was a teenager, and it had been her space. You only ever went in there if you were invited. I poked my head into the rooms along the hall as I made my way to the back of the house, and they were all the same as the lounge room. Dust-covered wooden floors, and bare walls. The windows were shut tight, and the curtains were closed to keep the light out.

The studio was the same when I opened the door. I had had my own space—you couldn't really call it a bedroom—on the verandah on the opposite side of the house. It had timber shutters that rolled down from the ceiling and I used to shut them to keep the weather— and the insects—out. Some nights, I'd leave them open while I got sleepy and I'd lie there and look up at the stars.

Aunty Vi had always told me that my Mum and Dad's spirits were up there in the stars, and some nights I had looked so hard that my eyes would ache and water.

I walked through the bathroom and smiled at the pink shower curtain that I had forgotten about. The door to the verandah was closed and I turned the handle and stepped into the room that had been mine.

My breath caught as I stared around. I blinked and my hand went automatically to the cord that I had used to pull to turn the light on, but of course there was no power.

The room was as I had left it when I went off to university. The bed still had a green chenille coverlet on it, and the bookshelf at the head of my bed was still full of my books. I walked to the end of the verandah and pulled open the curtains that covered the small window near the door that led out to the open verandah.

I shook my head. It was as though I had never left. My posters were still on the walls, and the teenage possessions I had left behind were still on the cupboard. Aunty Vi had believed me when I'd promised I'd come back one day. She must have instructed that my room remained untouched.

My legs trembled as I walked back to the bed and sat down and picked up the dog-eared copy of the *Magic Faraway Tree*.

Chapter 12

Tam

Tam looked across at Pippa. When they'd come back with the last load of boxes Pippa's eyes had been red; she'd obviously had a weep but had pulled herself together before the girls returned.

'Thanks for carrying it all in. I feel slack. Sit down for a while and I'll dig us out a cold drink.' Pippa went over to the eskies.

The three of them pitched in and by late afternoon, the house had been swept out, mould scrubbed away, swags set up, and now they were in the living room lit by half a dozen candles sitting on plates on an upturned box that had held some of the provisions. The eskies were in the kitchen, and the dry food had been stowed securely in a cupboard.

'Shame it's just the three of us sitting here tonight. It's quite romantic, isn't it, girls?' Tam said as she looked around. Pippa and Nell both looked tired and Pippa had a smudge of dirt on her nose.

Pippa snorted. 'I don't know about romantic; all I know is I'm tired.'

Nell held up her phone. 'It might be romantic but the only thing I'm worried about is how to charge my phone and my laptop.'

'Don't worry now. I'll get the generator going tomorrow. I've just got to put the diesel in and do something.' Pippa giggled.

'Do something?' Tam shook her head and chuckled. 'You've always been such a hands-on person, Pip.'

Pippa pulled a face at Tam. 'When I look at the generator tomorrow, I'm sure I'll remember what we used to do. If not, I'll get someone over from the mainland to show us.'

'Or I can Google it,' Nell offered.

Tam gestured to the eskies in the kitchen. 'We've got enough ice to last us for a couple of days and a swag each and we are on the island. What more could we ask for?'

Pippa raised her eyebrows. 'Electricity, real beds, and a plan.' She hesitated. 'And about a million other things I could think of if I wasn't so tired.'

'Well. I don't think we need to rush these things, do we, Nell?' Tam looked across the room. 'It's all about mindfulness. Living in the moment. And hey, what a real moment. On a tropical island with my two best friends and an exciting future to plan.'

Tam had shared her concern

about Pippa with Nell earlier when they'd carried the boxes up from the beach. Pippa had been sweeping the house out and Tam had voiced her concerns. They'd both promised to help keep her spirits up.

'I think it's a great idea and such a windfall for Pip, but I don't know whether she's put enough thought into it. I know her heart's in creating a resort here and that's what we have to trust and back her up.'

'It came too soon on top of Darren doing the dirty and losing her job,' Nell said. 'I worry that she's grasping at straws and letting her memories sway her.'

'Maybe.' Tam had nodded. 'Just look at it this way. She owns the house and half of this island. I think if we can help her settle emotionally and give her as much help as we can she'll be fine.' They linked fingers and made a pact before they came back to the house.

Tam looked across at Pippa now. Her face was shadowed in the flickering candlelight, but she looked calm. 'What do you girls fancy for dinner?' Tam pushed herself to her feet. 'What gourmet meal would you like me to whip up?'

Pippa waved a lazy hand. 'Surprise us.'

'Does anyone want a wine while I cook?' Tam asked crossing to the esky.

Pippa shook her head. 'Not for me. As soon as we eat, I'm going to crash. We've got a big day tomorrow. Cleaning up and lots of plans to make.'

'And don't forget you have to get the generator going,' Nell interjected

'Yes, getting the power going is a priority.' Pippa nodded and yawned at the same time. 'I shouldn't have got up so early this morning and gone for that run up to the lookout.'

Tam ferreted around in the kitchen and made them each a baguette with potato salad, pastrami and a dab of dressing from her special bottle she'd slipped into her luggage. She was looking forward to thinking about food again, and that gave her motivation to get in and help Pippa get the house cleaned up ready to start planning. Tam yawned and pushed her plate aside. 'I'd kill for a coffee.'

'Unless you feel like going out and lighting a fire, you're going to have to do without your coffee tonight, love,' Pippa said as she stood. 'We've got plenty of water, although I suppose we do need to conserve it until we can find out what we've got here.' She collected Tam and Nell's plates, and turned to the kitchen in the dim light. 'Once I get the power going, I'd like the three of us to sit down tomorrow and make a list of what we need to do first to make this place liveable, and then we'll start a feasibility study of whether the old place is worth doing up.'

Tam and Nell exchanged a worried glance as Pippa's voice trembled.

'Let's all call it a night. Pip, we'll have this place shipshape and up and running before we can blink. Not the resort; I mean, just for us to live here while we plan. Leave those plates. We'll clean up in the morning when we can see what we're doing.' Tam stood and yawned again. ' All this fresh air is killing me. Oh Pippa, I forgot to tell you.'

'Tell me what?'

Tam slapped a hand lightly against her forehead. 'How could I have forgotten? When we were at the shops at Hamilton Island on Friday, you'll never guess who I bumped into.'

'Chris Hemsworth,' Pip said with a grin.

Tam shook her head. 'I wish. No, it was Evie Bannister.'

'Evie from uni?'

'That's the one.'

'On holidays on Hamo?'

'No,' Tam's voice was excited. 'Would you believe she works there, and she told me to tell you if you're ever looking for anyone to help with the landscaping, she's available for contract work.'

'You told her about what we

were planning here?' Pippa frowned.

'No. I mean I didn't tell her that it was your resort. I said we were coming back here to do up your aunt's place, and she said if you were looking for a landscape gardener she could help out. It could be useful in a while.'

Pippa nodded. 'I always liked Evie. I've still got her number in my phone. I'll give her a call and see if she'd like to come out and have a look around in a week or two. It's one thing that we can get started without much cost. Just getting the tracks clear and planning where we can have our walks will be a good start to the outside and activities that we might plan.'

Tam was pleased when Pippa's shoulders straightened, and the spark came back into her eyes.

'So, tell me before we call it a night. What's your gut feeling? How you feel now that you're on the island? Do you still want to go ahead with this crazy plan of yours?'

'Crazy? Don't tell me you don't want to stay?'

Tam shook her head with a smile. 'I'm keen, but I think we should take a couple of weeks and have a bit of a break and let you settle.'

'What do you mean settle?'

'You've seemed a bit anxious, I guess. Just over the last few weeks, and a bit more before, when we came back with the boxes.'

Nell nodded. 'But if this is what you want, Tam and I are both happy to help and stay here with you.'

Pippa walked over and stood

beside her two friends. 'I love that you care about me enough to be worried, girls, but I've never been so sure of anything in my life.' She reached over and looped her arms around Tam and Nell's shoulders. 'Look at this place. Look at the potential, and more than that, for me, it's home. I'm really happy to be here. I just got a bit teary when I went back to my old room, and Aunty Vi had everything left there the way it used to be. I guess she always knew I'd come back one day.

'I want to do her proud and build up the best resort we can. No two weeks of thinking about it. I've made my mind up. Are you in?'

There was no hesitation as Tam and Nell looked at each other and nodded, before completing a circle with their arms.

'We're in.'

Chapter 13

Pippa

I woke up at dawn the next morning. I'd opted to leave my swag and I came into my old room and swept it out, opened the blinds and pulled down the flyscreens. I grabbed the light blanket out of my suitcase and put it on the bed.

Waking up in my childhood bed was a strange feeling, but a good one. I lay there for a few minutes watching the sunlight play on the wall. The leaves of the tree outside my room formed lacy patterns on the wall as the first breeze of the day puffed in. The winter season was ahead, and the prevailing winds were always from the southeast. A small gecko scurried across the ceiling as I watched, and I smiled wondering what other wildlife was in the house.

If there was one thing Nell hated it was critters of any sort. Spiders, snakes, cockroaches, bugs; I wondered how she'd cope in the tropics where they were all bigger and there were more of them. Before she'd climbed into her swag last night, she had shone her flashlight in all the dark corners of the living room and then scurried in, quickly zipping herself in.

'I feel quite safe in here,' she said. 'I might sleep in my swag even when we get the place sorted.' Tam and I had looked at each other and burst out laughing.

'I'm serious,' came the response from within the zipped-up swag.

'We can do mosquito nets,' I said.

'I'll think about it,' was the muffled response.

I'd blown the candles out and used the flashlight app on my phone; there was just enough light to make my way to the door. I slipped out onto the verandah and sat on the steps for a while before I'd headed to my bed. The sky was ablaze with stars and the only sound was the gentle wash of the water on the beach below us. It was as though the Gold Coast and my life down there had never happened.

I was so grateful to Nell and Tamsin for coming to the island. They had put their trust in me, and that was another reason to work hard and get this place up and running. The pressure that had been on me had dissipated. I hadn't missed Darren one bit and I realised what a lucky escape I'd had. I'd made some poor choices but the energy and passion I had put into my career down there was now going to be redirected, and it was up to me to make this venture succeed.

I smiled as I made my way along the verandah to my bed, excited about what the next weeks would bring.

I'd slept deeply and without dreaming, and when I woke, I felt renewed, full of life and energy and ready to face what the day would bring.

I climbed out of bed and pulled on a light cotton jumper and a pair of loose pants. My sneakers were by the door where I had left them, and I slipped into them and then pulled my hair back into a ponytail.

There was no sign of life in the living room from the two swags, just a light occasional snuffle from Tam's swag.

I opened the door quietly and

stepped out into the morning.

The air was clean and pure, and silence surrounded me. No sound of traffic roaring up the Gold Coast Highway, and no garbage trucks clanging and banging as they emptied bins.

With a smile I picked up a long stick and set off up the track. Now don't get me wrong, I wasn't going to attempt the mountain this morning, but there was a hill to the east overlooking the valley that also gave a spectacular view of the water.

I also had an ulterior motive. From the first hill I'd get a clear view of the new house that I'd seen across the bay when we came in on the boat yesterday. You couldn't see the house once you reached the sand, and I was curious about the other inhabitant of the island and how having a neighbour was going to pan out.

He might be a recluse, and he might not like what I was going to do, but there was nothing he could do to stop us.

At least I didn't think there was. I'd go over this afternoon and introduce myself.

It would be much better to introduce myself and start up an amicable relationship and have him happy with what we were planning on doing.

'Pollyanna,' I muttered to myself. 'And pigs might fly.' If what Jiminy had heard was correct we were in for a battle.

I grinned. And if there was one thing I had thrived on in the workplace and done very well in, it was developing strategies to get what I wanted.

I came to the place where the path to the mountain and Red

Wave Wall crossed the beach track, and I began to climb. Half an hour later I'd shed my cotton jumper and was down to my T-shirt and long pants. I reached the flat ledge halfway up the hill where I knew I'd get the first decent view of my neighbour's house.

I drew in a deep breath and my fingertips tingled with excitement as I turned to survey the vista in front of me.

It was too early for much water traffic out on the Whitsunday Passage, but in the distance, I could see a couple of catamarans heading south, their headsails white and billowing in the wind.

Another brilliant day beckoned as the sky and the sea melded together in a deep turquoise. A couple of fluffy clouds drifted in from the east, but they soon dissipated. I was surprised at how clear the track was. It had been more heavily vegetated when I'd lived here ten years ago; I wouldn't be surprised to find that our neighbour was using it. Either that or there'd been a lot of hikers or birdwatchers, but Jiminy had said very few came to the island now. I frowned as I remembered that there had been quite a few climbers attempting the peak and Red Wave Wall when I'd lived with Aunty Vi. Another market for our resort. Rock climbers, birdwatchers, and those who simply wanted to chill. I was even considering a spa idea; I had some great marketing ideas for a pamper package, and I knew there was a market there for that service.

Excitement sizzled through me as I thought of the different services our resort could offer.

I always thought of the project

in terms of *our* resort; it was going to be a group venture—Tam and Nell were as big a part of it as I was.

I turned slowly to look at the house on the hill opposite. For a moment I couldn't see it and then I nodded slowly.

Very clever.

The house had been built to blend into the environment. In fact, if you didn't know it was there you would probably glance around and not notice it nestled into the hillside. The timber work was a natural colour, and the roof was green. As I looked, I could see the shape of the building. The morning sunlight reflected off one window in a bright flash. There was no sign of life, but it was early, and most people wouldn't be up and about yet. I wondered if anyone lived there with him.

I sat on the wide rock ledge and drew my knees up to my chin. I wasn't going to worry about anything.

Worrying about a problem wouldn't change it, or make it go away. Aunty Vi had taught me that. She had made me confront my fears and talk about the things that mattered to me. And she'd taught me what was important. I think she would have been a bit disappointed in me over the past few years. I'd made some poor choices: Darren and the job I'd put all of my energy into.

Then again, she'd been astute, and we'd spoken regularly until she'd passed away. I knew she would have had a reason for leaving me half the island. And I wasn't going to let her down.

I let the beauty of the island seep into my soul and whispered under my breath 'Aunty Vi, I promise you that I'm going to make this a place you would have been so proud of.'

The sun climbed higher as I sat there, and finally it was the grumbling of my stomach that pushed me to move. I stood, ready to go back to the house and start work.

One last look at the beautiful view for the morning. I turned my head and scanned the water from south to north. A sea eagle swooped above me and then down to the water; my gaze followed it to a motor launch making its way past the island. As I stared out over the water the sound of stones rolling down the hill brought me out of my reverie.

I turned as the noise got louder, and I tensed, wondering if I was about to be confronted by one of the wild goats that had been on the island since being introduced, and then abandoned back in the 1930s.

There hadn't been many of them left when I'd lived here but we used to see the occasional one in the drier months as they foraged closer to the house for food. I stood back and waited, hoping it wasn't a buck because they could get quite nasty. My stomach gurgled again, but this time it was from nerves rather than hunger.

I frowned as the noise got closer. They weren't goat footsteps; there was somebody up the track and walking down the hill towards where I was standing. I glanced down to the beach, but there was no boat or tender pulled up onto the sand. I wondered whether there were hikers or birdwatchers who had come onto the island from the bay around the other side.

A man appeared around the bend in the track.

He pulled up short when he saw me, and my mouth dropped at the same instant that his eyes widened. A strange feeling rippled through me.

His voice was quiet as he came down the last small incline and stood beside me. 'Hello, so we meet again.' He didn't seem the slightest bit surprised that the woman he'd met on One Tree Hill yesterday morning was now on a hill on an island a few kilometres away from Hamilton Island.

The same man who had stared at me in the restaurant two nights ago.

'What are you doing on my island?' I asked, determined to take the upper hand. And if I was honest, I wanted to take control of the conversation because looking at him made me feel strange. 'Are you following me? And where's your boat?'

But it was as though I hadn't spoken.

'Can I ask you something?' he said. His eyes hadn't left mine, and heat ran into my face.

I wasn't scared of him. Somehow, I knew he represented no danger to me, but I still wanted to know what he was doing here. A suspicion half-formed in my mind as I looked back down at the bay and confirmed that there was no boat moored there. Only the black boat owned by my neighbour. 'After you answer my question. What are you doing here? It's a private island and really not available for casual day-trippers.'

'I know I could ask you the

same question.' His eyes were still intent on mine. 'What were you laughing about in the restaurant the other night. You and your friends?'

What was it with this guy? Had he thought we were laughing at him? Why did he want to know? Bizarre.

Without thinking the words tumbled from my lips. 'We were trying to think of a name for our—' I broke off. If he was who I thought he was, I wasn't going to tell him anything.

'For your . . .' he prompted.

'For my house.'

'Which house?'

'You are very curious, Mr—?'

He held out his hand and I took it reluctantly. My arm tingled as his fingers held mine.

'Rendell. Rafe Rendell. That is my house.' He gestured across the bay. 'And you are Pippa?'

I frowned and spoke slowly. 'Yes, Pippa Carmichael. How do you know who I am?'

'You're at Ma Carmichael's house?'

'I am.' I lifted my chin. 'Ma Carmichael? You knew my aunt?'

'I did. I met her before she moved away. She was a kind woman.' His eyes were distant now as though he was remembering Aunty Vi. 'I used to visit with her when my house was being built.' His voice faded and his eyes narrowed. 'She mentioned that she had a niece called Pippa who had lived here with her for a while.'

'Well that would be me.' I kept my eyes on him.

'I heard your friends call you the other night in the restaurant.'

'Well, Mr Rendell, she never once mentioned you, or the fact that you built a house on my island.'

His expression tightened. 'Your island?'

'Yes. My aunt has passed away, and I've inherited the island.'

'Not the island.' He shook his head. 'You may have had full access before. Maybe you're not aware of the fact that the island is now half mine. I don't want to share it with anyone, so I'm prepared to make you a very generous offer for the remainder.'

The remainder? Anger took root in my chest. He had totally dismissed the loss of Aunty Vi and wanted my island.

He could go take a flying leap.

The wind was picking up and even though we were in the tropics, it could be cold blowing off the water until the sun reached its zenith in the winter, and I crossed my arms.

'Oh, are you now?' I said.

Anyone who knew me well would have recognised the tone in my voice. That was the one thing that Darren had taken notice of. He knew when my voice lowered to that level, it was time to take a hike and let me have my say.

'Yes, I am,' he said. 'Very generous.'

I held his gaze for a moment or two and he didn't look away.

I turned my back and walked down the hill without another word, but I was conscious of his eyes on me the whole way. It was a relief when the path turned into the shaded forest.

So much for starting off in an amicable relationship, Pollyanna.

But my temper didn't cool at all.

So, he would make me a very generous offer, would he?

Pah! Mr Rafe Rendell could try, but if anyone left the island it wasn't going to be me.

Chapter 14

Pippa

'Now you have to loosen the bleed screw a couple of turns,' Nell read from the generator manual that we'd found in the shed behind the house.

Tam leaned forward and she was so close to me her hair brushed against my cheek.

'Tam, move back. You're blocking my light,' I said as she peered over my shoulder. 'Okay. Got that. What now, Nell?'

'Pump the primer pump until diesel fuel comes out of the loose bleed screw,' Nell said slowly. 'Sheesh, Pip. This might as well be written in Chinese. It means nothing to me.'

I pressed the soft rubber button in and out a few times and smiled as diesel trickled onto my fingers. 'It's okay. I remember now. Aunty Vi let the generator run out of fuel a couple of times and this is what she did.' I sat back and rocked on my heels. 'It'll start now, so stand back, gals.'

I pressed the start button and the sound of the motor purring was like music to my ears, and it even made up for the stink of the diesel that pervaded the air and covered my fingers.

I turned to look at Tam.

Her grin was as wide as mine and she high-fived me. 'You rock, girlfriend.'

Nell took off as soon as the generator fired. 'Ew, it stinks.'

I picked up a rag and wiped the fuel off my fingers. I hated the smell of diesel. As soon as I'd walked into the small shed, I'd wrinkled my nose at the pungent smell. But with that smell came good memories, and now we had a generator humming along, and with it, power to the house.

I gestured to the door and Tam followed me out into the fresh air. Nell was standing beside the clothes line.

'Now what?' she asked.

'Now we have electricity that means lights and power points.'

'And that means I can charge my phone!' Nell hurried towards the house.

By the time Tam and I reached the back steps, Nell was inside.

'And that means we can have a hot breakfast. If there is power, I can use that skillet pan that I saw in the pantry to cook us an omelette. What do you think?' Tam asked.

'Sounds good to me. First thing I'm going to do is have a wash.'

When I'd got back from my

walk up the hill, Tam and Nell had been up and dressed. The first thing I'd wanted to do was try to get the power going so we'd headed straight out to the shed.

I didn't tell them about my meeting with Mr Rafe Rendell straight up, as Nell was intent on telling me about the lizard that had been in the hallway when she'd headed to the bathroom.

'They're harmless, just skinks.' I said. 'You'll get used to them. And I'm sorry, it was my fault. I opened the blinds when I went to bed so I could see the stars. It would have come in that way.'

Getting the generator going had restored my confidence. I honestly thought that we'd have to get someone over to help us but doing it myself gave me a huge boost. Having power would make such a difference, but I had to remember to get enough diesel to keep it running. It would mean a trip over to Hamilton Island, or even a phone call to see if we could get a delivery. It was the sort of thing I'd taken for granted when I'd lived here. Aunty Vi had just kept things running, and I'd been oblivious to how it all came together. I didn't even recall her going to Hamilton Island or the mainland, and I guess she got stuff delivered back in those days.

Keeping my mind on those day-to-day problems we would face meant that I wasn't thinking about meeting my neighbour on the hill. He'd really pissed me off with his attitude and his plummy voice. He obviously thought he was something special.

I curled my fingers into fists and frowned as my nails cut into my skin. The bloody hide of him.

So, he wasn't prepared to share my island with me. He would buy it off me so he could have it all. Who the hell did he think he was?

Typical man. What was it about men these days? They were so bloody selfish. It was all about what *they* wanted.

What Jiminy had said about Rendell being rich must be true, because how many people would have enough money to offer to buy an island?

I pulled the bathroom door shut a little harder than I should, and it closed with a bang. I strode down the hallway and Nell looked up from where she was sitting on the floor in front of a double power point. Her laptop and her phone were already plugged in, and I could see the charging lights glowing.

'What are you looking so cross

about?' she asked with a frown. 'Is the power still on?' She leaned forward and looked at the phone.

'Power's fine,' I said. 'I was thinking about bloody men and how they always think they are so entitled.'

Her eyebrows shot up. 'Men? What men?'

'I met our neighbour when I went for my walk.'

Tam came in from the kitchen wiping her hands on a tea towel.

'The mysterious neighbour?'

I nodded. 'Yep, we only have the one. Thank God.'

'Did you go over there?' Tam turned back towards the kitchen door. 'Come in here and tell me about it, I've got butter melting in the pan. I just came to tell you both that I've boiled the jug and we have coffee.'

Nell stood and we both

followed Tam into the kitchen. The smell of chopped onion and herbs filled the kitchen with an enticing aroma and my mouth watered.

'Sit.' Tam pointed to the kitchen table.

We both did as directed, and I smiled as Tam slipped a cup of coffee across to me.

'Now, tell us about this guy.'

'I was on the hill when I heard footsteps. He was out walking on the hill too, and he came past where I was standing checking out his house.'

'Embarrassing.'

'No, not at all. I have a right to go wherever I want on my side of the island.'

'So what's he like?' Tam asked as she cracked eggs into the pan.

'I guess the old maxim would fit. Tall, dark and handsome.'

'Interesting,' Nell said.

I shook my head. 'No, he's arrogant. I didn't like him.' I cupped my hands around the coffee mug and inhaled. 'And he thinks he's going to buy my half of the island.'

'Really! What did you say?' Tam lifted the wooden spoon and looked across at me.

'Nothing. I gave him a very cold look, bid him a good day, and headed back here.'

'Hmm, a good neighbourly start,' Nell said.

'I'm not sorry. He started it. And he said he'd met Aunty Vi too.'

'So he's been here a while then?' Tam narrowed her eyes as she flipped the omelette.

'Apparently.'

Nell picked up her mug. 'I suppose you have to look at it from his viewpoint. He's paid a fortune to buy his own island—'

'Uh uh.' I shook my head. 'Nell, It's not *his*. It's been in my Mum's family for almost a hundred years. He's bought a bit of it and built a house. I can't believe Aunty Vi sold off a portion of the island and didn't tell me.'

'Who wants toast?' Tam lifted the pan from the stove. 'I found the toaster in the pantry. Pippa, did you ever consider she might have done it to fund her move to the aged care facility? It meant she didn't have to sell the house and was able to keep that for your family and at least half the island. I'm sorry, chicky, but I think you're going to have to get used to having him here.'

I sipped my coffee. 'I'm going to go to see him and sort it out this afternoon. The sooner he knows that we're here to stay, the better. He might decide to go.'

'Did you find out his name?' Nell pushed her chair back. 'I'll get my laptop and Google him. If he's rich enough to buy half a tropical island there should be some mention of him somewhere.'

I waited until she came back to the table. 'Rafe Rendell.'

'Sexy name,' Tam said. 'How old is he?'

'You've already seen him. He was in the Italian restaurant the other night with a blonde woman. The one with the real diamond clip in her hair.'

Tam and Nell both looked at me blankly as Nell opened her laptop.

'Nope, didn't take much notice of who was in there. We were having fun deciding names for the resort,' Tam said. 'So how old?'

I shrugged. 'Maybe this side of forty.'

'And he has a wife here too?'

'I've got no idea. Whoever she was, I did notice they seemed to be fighting over dinner.'

'Ooh,' Tam said as she slid three loaded plates onto the table. 'More and more interesting.'

'I can't believe that neither of you noticed him.'

They both looked at me.

'You obviously did,' Nell said.

'I like observing others.' Heat ran up into my face.

'Especially good-looking others,' Tam said with a giggle. 'I'm quite looking forward to meeting our neighbour.'

'Can't find him.' Nell clicked on her keyboard with one hand and picked up her fork with the other. 'I'll have to try a deeper search strategy.'

Nell was our IT guru. If there was anything to be found on Rafe

Rendell, she wouldn't give up until she'd discovered it.

'Jiminy said there was talk he was a movie star, didn't he?' Tam joined us at the table. I smiled. She'd found a tablecloth in the pantry and had put a sprig of wild parsley in a jar in the centre of the table.

'That was gossip, I think,' I said.

Nell nodded as she forked omelette from her plate. 'Yep, all gossip. I've found him. I think.' She turned the screen so I could see it. 'This is a Rafe Rendell from England. He's got dark hair and he's a chartered accountant from Oxford. Is that your Rafe?'

I burred up. 'He's not *my Rafe*.'

'You know what I mean,' Nell said. 'Is that him?'

I peered at the screen. 'I think it is, but he looks way younger there.'

Tam leaned over. 'Show me.'

When Nell obliged, Tam nodded. 'Wow. He is a good looker. Movie star looks.'

'That photo was taken fifteen years ago. It was in staff photo files of a company. Now that I've found an image and you *think* that could be him, I can run a reverse image search, and it should pull up any other photos without his name in the text. If there's any more to be found, that is.' Nell put her fork down and her fingers clicked on the keyboard.

'That's all Chinese to me,' I parrotted Nell's words when she had read the generator manual.

'We each have our skills.' She flashed a grin my way. 'You got the power going. I can find our neighbour on the internet. Give me ten minutes.'

All was quiet as we ate, and Nell focused on her laptop.

'That was yum, thank you, Tam.' I pushed my plate away and sat back. 'Okay, now that we've seen the place, I'd like to make a list of what we need to do and allocate some jobs to each of us. Are you cool with that?'

Tam nodded. 'As long as I can fit a swim in somewhere. That reminds me. There's no sign of any boat here.'

'I know. I thought of that when I was going to sleep last night. It's the one thing I must sort quickly. We can't be isolated here.'

Tam leaned back in her seat. 'Speaking of skills, what part of the house do you want to start with, Pip? Have you got any ideas about the general layout of the resort?'

'I have.' I'd been thinking about that before my encounter on the hill earlier. I reached over and pulled over the notebook that I'd put on the table earlier and opened to a blank page. Picking up a pencil I quickly sketched the shape of the bay where we'd got off Jiminy's boat yesterday, and then put a square where the house was.

I grinned as I sketched. Having those new pencils each school year of my childhood had developed an ability to draw. Although maybe it had been there all the time, and my mum had known that.

I put the tip of the lead pencil on the curve of the bay. 'I was thinking about starting small and exclusive. Maybe half a dozen huts similar to the ones we stayed in at Hamilton Island. You know, like Lord Howe Island. A maximum number of guests.'

Nell looked up; she'd been listening as she searched. 'Will that be feasible financially? Every accommodation company I've done the books for over the years, says it's bums in beds that counts.'

Tam giggled. 'And if you only have a small number of beds, that's not many bums in beds.'

'True. Maybe, I'd better rethink the small, because we're going to have to hire staff.'

'What about the house? Are you going to make that part of the resort?' Tam asked.

'I've got two ideas. First one is to develop the kitchen and living room here into the restaurant. You'll need to tell me what you'll need. It'll mean that we'd have to live at the back of the house, and that could be a problem as we get more staff.'

'Maybe. What's the other option?'

'An entirely separate guest

area down on the bay. I know if I'm on holidays I like to be able to see the water, so I was thinking about the kitchen adjacent to the huts with a big outdoor restaurant. You know, like the huts on a bigger scale? Flag stones on the floor, and no walls.'

'Have you thought that out? What about the furniture being exposed to the weather? And the bar? You'd have to be able to lock it up.'

'There used to be a resort over on Long Island like that when I was in my teens,' I said. 'I went over there for a sixteenth birthday party once and it stuck in my mind. We called it Gilligan's. There were little wallabies hopping around and birds wandering through. It was like an outside barbeque area, but I think we could do it in an upmarket way.' I had sketched what I was imagining as I described it and Tam leaned closer and nodded.

'I like the idea and it would be great from a marketing point of view. But I'm sure you've already got a handle on that.' Her blonde curls bounced as she nodded. 'This is going to be so much fun.'

'And a lot of hard work,' I said.

'Jackpot,' Nell interrupted, and we turned to her. 'More than three hundred images of him, but not one with the name Rafe Rendell on it.'

'Three hundred? Why would someone have three hundred photos online?' I said.

'Someone famous?' Tam ventured.

'Do you think it's the same guy?' I asked.

'Come around and have a look, and you tell me. You're the one who's seen him in the flesh.'

Tam and I both stood and walked around the table to look at Nell's laptop screen.

The screen was filled with photos of the man I'd encountered on the hill an hour ago. The same dark hair falling over his eyes. Eyes with that same intense blue-eyed stare looked out from the large photo in the centre. It captured his face perfectly.

'That's him. Exactly. It could have been taken this morning.' I swallowed. 'So, he is famous?'

I really hoped he wasn't, but my confidence in that being the case had plummeted. Famous usually meant rich. And rich would mean that he would have the resources to fight the resort being developed on the island.

Nell shook her head and zoomed out. 'Well, if it's the same guy he has a different name. That's a photo of Jack Smith on the back cover of his book that came out two years ago.'

'Jack Smith, the author?'

'Yes.' Tam nodded. 'It's *the* Jack Smith who wrote that book that was made into a movie last year. The one like a James Bond movie, but different. The hero was softer.'

'*The Legacy*,' I said. 'I saw it at the movies with Darren.' As much as I hated to admit it, *The Legacy* was one of the best movies I had seen in recent years, and I'd bought the DVD when it came out.

'Yes, that's the name of this book. The photo is on the book jacket. So, you think it's him?'

'It has to be unless he has a twin.' I leaned closer and a shiver ran down my spine. 'Jiminy said one of the gossip thingies was that he was an author. I guess he was right.'

'Maybe this is where he writes and why he's so focused on privacy?'

'He introduced himself as Rafe Rendell, so maybe he has a doppelganger? But whoever he is, I have no idea what he does here. We barely spoke.'

'He certainly is a looker.' Tam said. 'If you had a name like that why on earth would you write a book under the name, Jack Smith?

'I have no idea.' I shrugged.

'Do you want me to open some of the articles about him, so you can read them, Pip?' Nell looked across at me, but I shook my head.

'No. I don't care what he does or what he calls himself. I'm not selling my half of the island to Rafe Rendell or Jack Smith, whoever he is.'

'Maybe if you find out more

about him, you'll know what you're up against.' Nell was always smart.

'No. I know what media spin is. Whatever is written about him will be purely to sell his books or feed the gossip machine.' I tapped my finger against my lips as I thought. 'I'll see him later today. But first, my lovelies, we have some work to do.'

Chapter 15

Rafe

I spent the morning staring at a blank page, but despite the screen remaining empty of words, for the first time in months thoughts swirled around and ideas came in thick and fast. At the same time, along with the plot lines that were fighting to come to the fore, was the image of the woman I'd now encountered three times. If I put those encounters in a book, Jenny—my editor—would say that it was an unlikely coincidence. The seeing her three times, I mean.

But no matter what Jenny would have said about that is a story, I would have kept it there. I'd learned to follow my heart with my stories, and my readers were loyal.

Those readers I was letting

down by not producing the next decent book.

Jenny had stopped forwarding the reader emails, in a bid to let me "find myself". That was what she'd called it when I'd first moved to the island.

I looked down at my hands and slowly flexed my fingers. It was a process to get the thoughts from my head onto a keyboard and into a semblance of a story on the screen. Once, it had been easy and I hadn't appreciated the ease with which I'd done it.

When I had moved to the island, I had hoped that ability would return, but I had spent more than two years wasting time and feeling sorry for myself. Words had come easily, but when they formed a story, they had been bitter, and somehow, whatever I wrote had been tainted by the hurt and emptiness inside me. And now, just when the positive ideas were coming back, my solitude had been interrupted. I didn't dare think that there was a connection between the beautiful niece of my elderly friend, and the surge of positivity that was making my fingers tingle.

I wondered how long Pippa Carmichael— who seemed to be stuck in my thoughts—was going to stay here. I'd seen two others get off the boat yesterday— obviously her companions at the restaurant the other night— and I knew they had to be staying in the old house although it had stayed in darkness last night. The occasional flicker across the bay had told me that they were relying on candlelight.

Hopefully that would mean that they wouldn't stay long, and I could go back to my peaceful existence. She'd been rude and the fact that she said she'd inherited half of the island didn't sit comfortably with me. Even though I was sorry that Ma had passed on, I wasn't happy about sharing the island with anybody.

No matter how beautiful she was.

Life had taught me that women were not to be trusted. Behind the most beautiful façade and loving exteriors, there was always a self-centred shrew who wanted her own way. I had to keep that to the forefront of my mind.

Jenny had told me to wake up to myself, but she didn't know anything about my life before I had begun to write. I wasn't going to dwell on that either.

I pushed the beautiful ginger-haired owner of the other half of the island out of my thoughts and focused on the ideas that were vying for my attention. My fingers began to click on the keyboard, and I let myself become lost in an imaginary world. An imaginary world where the bitterness had left, and there was hope for the future

##

A long time later, the growling of my stomach brought me back to the present. I glanced at the time on the bottom right of the computer screen and was surprised to see it was late afternoon. I glanced to the left of the screen and was even more surprised to see that I'd written six thousand words.

A reluctant smile tugged at my mouth as I stood and stretched. It might be a crap story, but at least I'd made a decent start and the relief that brought was indescribable.

I made my way to the kitchen and made a sandwich and ate it as I stared out over the water. Already the next chapter was nagging at me, but I needed to get some fresh air, and I needed to stretch my muscles. I grabbed a bottle of water from the fridge and headed outside. The clouds had blown in from the south east, and there was a smell of rain in the air.

I tried not to be concerned about the occupants of the house across the bay, but I couldn't help my gaze lingering as I headed for the track.

Apart from my boat, the bay was deserted and there was no sign of life. I hoped that as I'd worked, a boat had come in and whisked away the unwanted visitors. A slight pang of regret settled in my chest. I had sort of enjoyed talking to Ma Carmichael's niece.

Even though her reaction to my offer to buy the rest of the island had not gone down well.

I looked up and was surprised to see the woman in my thoughts walking on the path towards me.

It was almost magical, as though I had conjured her up, and I blinked to clear my vision.

She stopped walking and stared at me.

'I thought you'd gone,' I said. I knew I sounded rude this time, even though I hadn't meant to.

Her hands went to the hips and her chin lifted. 'And where would I be going to?'

I stared, letting my eyes roam over her features. Her face was beautiful, even as her brow wrinkled in a frown.

'I assumed you wouldn't be

staying long,' I said.

'Well, you assumed wrong, and really, is how long I stay any of your business?'

I bristled. 'Perhaps not my business, but I would like to know what's going on, on my island.'

Her eyes flared with temper, and I could see her fighting to control it. 'I believe we had this discussion this morning.'

'Perhaps we did, but that doesn't counter the fact that you are trespassing.'

The hold on her temper failed. 'Trespassing?' she spluttered.

'Yes, this track is on my land.'

She looked around. 'I see no boundary, and I find it hard to believe that my aunt would have sold the land with access to Red Wave Wall and the mountain.'

'This is my land. I own down to the glade where the two paths join.

So technically you are trespassing.'

'So, if I want to climb the mountain, I can't?' Her eyes narrowed as she challenged me.

'That's correct. Unless you asked politely, and I granted permission to you to walk on the part of the track that is on my land.' I was beginning to enjoy myself. Her olive skin now had a tinge of red on her cheeks, and when she wasn't talking, her lips were set in a straight line.

'Well, I'm going to have to request that you hand that bit of land back to me, as I will need access to the mountain.'

'There are other walks on the island,' I said to be difficult. It didn't bother me to have her use the track, but it was interesting pushing her buttons and getting a reaction.

'My guests will want to climb

the mountain.'

'You're being joined by more people?'

'Eventually,' she said with a narrow smile. 'I was actually on my way over to your house to talk to you about that.'

'Eventually? You are having more friends join you?' I repeated dully as the prospect of my peaceful solitude was shattered. 'How long do you intend holidaying on the island?'

'Oh, it's no holiday, Mr Rendell. I've moved back home, and I'm here to stay. I'll need access to this land for my guests.'

'Guests?' A suspicion was beginning to form in my mind. 'When you say guests, I am getting the impression you're not talking about friends who might come to stay.'

'Oh, you are very astute. I am

talking about *paying* guests. Guests who will be staying at my *resort* on Pentecost Island.'

'What!'

'I would like to have a conversation, and come to an agreement. Perhaps we could go to your house?'

'The only agreement I'm interested in is buying the island from you.' I stared at her for a long moment. She held her chin high and didn't break eye contact.

This time, it was me who turned away. I didn't care if she thought I was rude. The only thing I cared about was the fact that my idyllic life here was at risk.

Idyllic? a voice nagged at me. Far from idyllic if the truth be known.

No way was there going to be a resort on *my* island. Boatloads of people disturbing my peace, walking on my tracks and interrupting my solitary existence. Stickybeaks peering at my house; it wouldn't be long before they realised who I was. I'd had enough of the hordes peering at my little cottage back home in England before I'd headed to the tropics.

I would fight any move she made. I didn't care what it cost.

Her voice followed me as I headed down the track. 'When you regain your temper, Mr Rendell, come over to the house. I'd like to talk some more.' The wind caught her words, but I'd heard enough. I ignored her and kept walking.

I was sure I heard a laugh follow me into *my* rainforest.

Chapter 16

Pippa

'That's so good of you, Jiminy. Are you sure you have time to take me over?'

I was at the marina on Hamilton Island. We'd been on Pentecost Island for five days and had started to run out of supplies, and diesel for the generator was getting low so I'd called Jiminy. He'd collected the three of us from the island early this morning and brought us across the passage. Tam and Nell had headed off to the general provisions store to stock up on food.

The good news was that Jiminy had located Aunty Vi's launch in storage on one of the back wharves of the working marina.

'Old Ma—I mean your aunt— obviously paid to have it

maintained, Pip,' he said as we walked past the workshops on our way over to the back wharf. 'The launch might be old but she's in tip top condition.'

'Excellent. We won't need to trouble you to take us back.'

'It's no trouble. You're sure you're right to take her across to Pentecost already?'

I looked up at the sky. There was barely any wind and the forecast that I'd seen on the board as we'd walked off the tourist wharves was for a still and fine day. 'I'll be fine. I used to take her out when I lived here, with no trouble and in seas rougher than this. I'll get you to come on board with me while I make sure I remember everything, and then we'll be fine.' I turned to him with a frown. 'I did notice it took you three attempts to get into the bay at the island the other day though. That's my only worry.'

'Maybe you could get your neighbour's permission to take it into this jetty?'

'Hmm. Maybe.' I shrugged. 'I guess the worst he can do is say no after I go in there. We'll unload and then I'll take her around to Back Bay and put her on a mooring if he says no.'

'Sounds like you've got it all sorted then.'

I nodded. Even though we'd only been on the island five days, we'd achieved a lot. Nell had been online every day, as well as making many calls. She knew exactly what approvals we needed before we opened the resort, and she already had the paperwork underway.

Tam and I had chuckled when Nell had removed the small

portable printer and scanner from her suitcase, but it had been worth its weight in gold this week. Nell had printed out the forms, I'd signed them, and they'd been scanned and sent off to the various relevant bodies.

We'd already had an email reply from the local Tourism Board who'd been excited to hear of our proposal.

Let us know when you're up and running and we'll do a feature.

Woo hoo! That had been a bottle of bubbles night.

We were all tired and pleased to have a day away from the house. Tam and I had scrubbed the house from top to bottom and I planned to get our furniture out of storage, and have it sent over as soon as we could organise delivery. We'd cleared the path from the steps to the track, and I'd mown the grass at the back of the house with the ancient mower I'd used as a teenager. I could feel a little bit of the happiness growing in me, and the person I'd been at the Gold Coast seemed to be fading more every day.

So far we'd had a dream run, and were moving a lot faster than I'd thought was possible.

The only fly in the ointment was our neighbour.

I was so deep in thought I almost bumped into Jiminy when he stopped in the middle of a finger wharf.

'There she is, Pippa.' He pointed to the boat rocking gently in the wash from a boat that was going past.

Nostalgia flooded though me as I looked at the classic lines of the old launch. If I closed my eyes, I could imagine Aunty Vi at the helm in her faded green hat and her fishing shirt. She'd been such a character and I had loved her so much. Again, regret spiked though me; I had walked away from that life.

'I should have come back to see her,' I said quietly. 'Aunty Vi, I mean.'

Jiminy looked at me and I could see he understood. 'It's called life, Pip. It often gets in the way of what we should do. You're back now, and I know that's what she would have wanted.'

I nodded. 'It is. And I am going to work my butt off to build a successful resort on the island.' I put my hands on my hips and turned to him. 'And I don't care if it's a bad marketing move. I'm going to call our resort Ma Carmichael's.'

'Good on you, and I like it. Ma

Carmichael's has a ring to it.'
Jiminy's teeth flashed in a wide
grin. 'Come on, let's get you on
board and see if you can really
remember how to steer a boat.'

My hands stayed on my hips as
I accepted the challenge. 'Bring it
on, Jim.'

By the time Tam messaged me
to see where to get the groceries
sent to, I was easing the launch
into the wharf near Jiminy's boat.
I'd convinced him that I knew what
I was doing. I'd taken the launch
out of the marina, done a couple of
quick circuits of the bay, and a
longer trip over to Dent Island.

'Not bad for a landlubber,' he
said as I eased the launch up to
the concrete wharf and he dropped
the fenders.

'Hey, I'm an old salt from way
back,' I protested with a grin.

As Jiminy jumped off, Tam and

Nell appeared carrying four bags of groceries each.

'You should have waited for me. They look heavy,' I said.

'There's a few more. You can come on the next trip.'

'No prob,' I said. 'I still have to get a drum of diesel too.'

'Having a boat is going to make life a lot easier. You'll have to teach Nell and I how to drive it,' Tam said as she held the bags out to me. 'This will make it a bit easier.'

'Absolutely,' I replied, pleased that Tam had offered.

'See you later,' Jiminy called as he headed over to his boat. 'You call me if you need anything.'

'Thanks, mate.' I waved back and he disappeared below deck on his boat.

Nell reached into one of the bags and passed over a couple of envelopes. 'A couple of replies already,' she said.

'Thanks for getting it, Nell,' I said. We'd organised for our forwarded and any new mail to be left at the post office on Hamilton Island, but I was surprised to see that there was some after only five days. I glanced down at the two envelopes. One was from the local council, but the other was from Morton and Morton, Aunty Vi's solicitor.

As Tam and Nell came aboard, I slit the envelopes open. The one from the council was an acknowledgement of our application to develop the resort.

'Four weeks, the council says,' I grinned. 'Until we have a go ahead.'

'Fantastic.' Nell's smile was as wide as mine.

'Thanks to you, Nell. I'd still be

trying to find out what to do. Appreciate it.' I opened the second envelope.

My mouth opened in disbelief as I quickly scanned the contents, and my stomach clenched as anger kicked in.

'Bloody hell. Who does he think he is!'

Nell was standing beside me. 'Who? The solicitor?'

'No, our neighbour. He's already made an offer on the house and my half of the island.'

'That was fast. A good one?' Tam frowned as she came across to stand next to Nell.

'I have no idea,' I spluttered. 'He wants to meet and talk. I don't care if he offers me a million dollars, it's not for sale.'

'We've only been there a few days,' Tam said as she read over my shoulder.

'And we've left him in peace. If anyone's leaving the island, he can go.' My hands trembled as I read the brief letter. 'It looks like he wants to make this very hard. Last time I spoke to him, he walked away from me.'

'Looks like he doesn't want to play fair,' Tam said.

'Or share. Looks like he wants the whole island,' Nell added.

'He might be famous, he might be rich, and he might want my island, but he's a jerk,' I said stuffing the letter into my bag. 'And you know what. I'm not going to let him bother me.'

'Good girl,' Nell said quietly.

'Come on, let's go finish and go home.'
##

It was only a thirty-minute trip across the water from Hamilton Island to home. It was closer to

Lindeman Island but that was another resort that had closed down over the past few years. I'd been encouraged by the letter from the Tourism board; they had expressed their pleasure at the proposal.

"Since the cyclone and the recent shark attacks, the media has focused on our region, and tourism has dropped off," the manager had written. *"If you need any assistance at all, please contact me. There are a number of grant initiatives available for application this winter."*

I'd been thinking about the focus of our development, and I was keen to get over to the mainland and meet with the manager.

'What do you think about a trip to Airlie Beach tomorrow?' I turned to Nell and Tam as we came around the northern point of the island. 'We could get our gear booked onto the barge and get the place organised.'

Neither of them answered. Tam was out of earshot, and Nell was engrossed on her phone screen. I didn't bother asking again as my eyes moved to the bay ahead. I'd watched Jiminy bring his boat in the other day, but that had been at high tide. The tide was ebbing now, and the water was swirling in eddies around the coral heads. If I tried to go in close to our place, there was a good chance I'd hit the coral and then we would be in trouble.

There was no choice. I looked ahead to the jetty on the other side of the bay and headed into the enemy's territory.

Uh oh . . .

Said enemy happened to be

sitting at the edge of the wharf. He stood as the launch approached and I swallowed back the hope that tried to wheedle its way in. He looked like a normal guy; his stance was relaxed and casual. Cut-off ragged denim shorts, a loose white long-sleeved shirt that gave him a rakish air.

'Oh my God. He's even better looking than he was in the photos. Look at those legs,' Tam breathed out in a hushed voice.

I couldn't help it. I looked at Nell and we both giggled.

'Down, girl,' I said. 'Remember the last guy whose legs you salivated over?' Tam had met Tyrone on a dating app, and that date hadn't had a good ending. He'd taken her to watch his wife in a triathlon—the wife she hadn't known about.

Poor Tam. She was always

looking for happiness. She needed to learn—like I had—that there were other ways to find happiness.

'Don't even think about it, Tam,' I warned as the launch approached his jetty.

I may as well have not spoken. As we got closer, she picked up the rope and my neighbour had no choice but to catch it.

'Thanks.' Tam's voice was cheery as she slid over the side of the launch onto the jetty. As I concentrated on easing the vessel up against the jetty, I was aware of her chatting away to him. Once I turned the motor off, I walked along to the bow and jumped onto the jetty. Nell was also standing with them by the time I got off the boat.

Glittering eyes locked with mine over Tam's head.

'Afternoon,' I said in the friendliest tone I could muster. 'We've come in on the wrong tide and I was hoping you'll let us unload here for a few minutes and then I'll take the boat around to Back Bay.'

Rafe—or Jack, whatever moniker he went by—walked across to where I was standing, and I couldn't believe it when he actually smiled at me. With a wave of elegant fingers at the boat, he nodded.

'Leave it there until the tide's up. Or for as long as you need to. There's plenty of room for two boats.'

I stared at him, but he kept smiling. Was this the same man I'd had two difficult conversations with? I narrowed my eyes; maybe he was trying the "be nice" approach. After all his letter to my solicitor was in the boat behind me.

Yes, that's what it was. I knew exactly what he was up to.

Tam walked across. 'I've just invited Rafe over for dinner.'

I tried to keep my mouth shut but I failed. 'What?'

And?

He must have been a mind reader. 'I'd be delighted to join you and get to know my neighbours.'

Suspicion vied with determination as I looked at him. He could be as co-operative and friendly as he liked, but there was no way he was getting his greedy hands on my half of the island.

'I got your letter,' I said tersely. 'The answer is no. So, there's no need to waste your time coming over for dinner.'

'Pippa!' Nell's keep-the-peace voice at any cost was horrified.

'It won't be a waste of time.' His voice was smooth. If he thought his sexy voice and perfect looks—and his money— were going to sway me, he was way off track.

I shrugged and mumbled under my breath. 'Whatever. Your time to waste.'

The three of them continued to have a conversation as I climbed back on board and collected the first of the grocery bags.

And the mail.

The drum of diesel would have to stay until I figured out how we'd get it up to the house.

But that was the least of my problems.

'So, Pippa. It looks like you're going to be staying a while.' The suave voice of my biggest problem followed me as I lugged the grocery bags along the wharf.

'Very perceptive,' I said

tersely.

'Here let me,' he said.

I stopped and looked at him. 'What exactly are you doing?'

Satisfaction rippled through me as his expression changed when he turned away from Nell and Tam.

'Being a gentleman.' Despite Rafe's friendly tone, his eyes were hard and cold. 'I was going to carry the bags for you.'

'No need. We're—I'm—fine.'

Nell rolled her eyes at me as she held her hand out for one of the bags. I shook my head and put them down at the end of the wharf. It only took me a couple of minutes to secure the launch and I ignored the conversation that continued at the other end of the jetty.

And the occasional laughter. Honestly, Tam and Nell were supposed to be on my side. I gave the last rope an extra hard tug, picked up more grocery bags and headed up the beach to the track.

Nothing was more satisfying than being a martyr.

Again, I was conscious of his gaze boring into my back—and my bare legs—as I walked away. Why was it that I was always walking away from this guy knowing he was staring after me? Why couldn't he just leave me in peace and let me get on with getting my life back on track on my island?

I struggled along the track with the heavy bags.

What the heck had the girls bought?

Eventually the sound of hurrying footsteps reached me from the track behind and I paused. Tam came up behind me.

'Here, stupid, give me one of those bags. Honestly, Pip, you can be so precious sometimes.'

'Precious!' I wheeled around to face her. 'What the hell do you mean by that?'

'Forget it,' Tam said, but I was on a roll now and I was ready to have a go. It felt good to let my simmering temper out.

'What the hell are you thinking inviting *him* for dinner tonight?'

'You don't get it, do you, Pip? Honestly, no wonder—' She broke off and looked at me as we trudged along the overgrown track to the house.

'Keep going,' I said coldly. 'No wonder what? You said "honestly". So be honest. Spit it all out.'

'Okay, I was going to say no wonder you had all that drama with Darren, and he let you down. No wonder Eric shafted you. You don't listen and you don't think. You don't read people.'

'I'm reading *you* loud and clear

now,' I spat out.

'Okay. So listen to me. What's the best way to find out what Rafe is doing?'

'So it's Rafe now, is it?' I widened my eyes at her, and fluttered my eyelashes.

'Jeez, Pip, listen to yourself.'

'Why did you invite him over? He's the enemy.'

'You don't think you are being overly dramatic?'

I shook my head and then stopped. 'Maybe a bit.'

'I invited him so you two can sit down and have an honest conversation about the situation. The worst that can happen is that he will go away and still want to buy the island. The best thing that can happen is that he might see your point of view.'

'Or I might see his? Is that what you're saying. You told me to wait a couple of weeks when we got here. Have you changed your mind about staying, because if you have, just go. That's fine by me.'

'No, that's not what I meant at all. I know what this place means to you, and I'm on board with the project one hundred percent. That's why you—with our help— have to sort the situation out now. It will be much better doing it face to face rather than through lawyer's letters.'

I looked at her and didn't comment.

'Pip?' Tam put the bag down and held out one hand.

'Probably,' I conceded.

'After all, the island has been in your family for many years. How long?'

I shrugged. 'Since about the 1930s.'

'And that's a bloody long time,'

Tam said. 'I'm totally with you. You need to keep it in your family and do what you want to do with the resort, but, girlfriend, you need to learn how to go about things.'

I sighed and squeezed her hand. 'I'm sorry for snapping, Tam. And yes, I know what you mean. I make poor choices, I'm lousy at reading people.'

She shoulder-bumped me and reached down to pick up the bag. 'But you're pretty damn good at picking friends.'

'I am,' I said with a smile. 'This is so important to me, so tell me why I should be nice to the guy?'

Tam shook her head as Nell came up behind us.

'Are you pair fighting?'

We both shook our heads this time.

'No, we're not fighting,' I said.

'Tam's just giving me a lesson on being sensible.'

'About time.'

'Thanks, Nell.' I rolled my eyes so she could see it.

'I think it was a great idea for Tam to invite him for dinner. He seems like a nice guy and he said to tell you to leave the boat there.'

'What?'

'He said to tell you there's no need to move it. He really doesn't mind if you leave it at his wharf.'

Shock filled me. 'Did he say that?'

Nell nodded. 'Yeah, he seems like a really nice guy. A real gentleman.'

If I was honest, I had to admit that he had mostly been polite when I was talking to him. It was just that blasted letter that had got beneath my skin. And the way he'd turned his back at me. But to be fair, I'd done exactly the same thing to him.

Nell held her hand out for the third grocery bag and Tam chuckled as we made our way towards the house.

'My God, how about that sexy English accent?' she said. 'I almost swooned. He's a Colin Firth voice double!'

I smiled. 'You're hopeless, Tam. Don't go having a romance with our neighbour.' My smile widened as I turned to her. 'Then again, if it's the only way to keep the island it might be worth a shot.'

'Nope, I'm happy to look and listen. He's way too cultured for me.'

Even though we all laughed as we walked back to the house, I was still smarting inside from Tam's words.

#

Tam and I had been prone to arguments since our primary school days, and Nell had always been the peacekeeper, but there was no need for her to intervene this afternoon. Tam and I had made our peace, but I knew it was still fragile. Had I made a mistake inviting them to come with me?

I stuck my head into the kitchen as the smell of garlic tickled my nose.

'I'm going out to the back garden for a while. I want to get the herb garden ready so I can buy some plants when we go over to the mainland.'

'Make sure you're here for dinner.' Tam put the saucepan she'd been lifting down onto the sink. 'Pip?'

'Yes?'

'Are we good?'

I nodded slowly. 'You were hard on me, but I guess I deserved it. And yes, we're good.' I headed out the back door to the garden.

I knew Tam would be upset if she knew my intention *was* to be absent when our neighbour arrived. I'd avoid that stand-around, have-a-drink, social chit chat before we sat at the table. I'd come in for dinner, and then as soon as we'd finished eating, I would find an excuse to go to my room. I wanted to make some calls anyway. That would be a good excuse. No one had asked me whether it suited me to be neighbourly tonight.

I'd endure the meal, and try to keep my temper, but I didn't have to spend the whole evening in his company. I would ring Evie and see if she had some time to come across and talk about expanding the walking tracks on my side of the island.

Yes, I had it all sorted. What was it they said about the best laid plans? Would I ever learn?

Chapter 17

Pippa

My plan backfired spectacularly. The light was fading fast but I'd spent a good two hours digging, clearing, and laying garden beds edged with some old timber lengths that I'd found behind the shed. I turned them all over carefully before I dragged them over. Despite what I'd said to Nell, the last thing I wanted was to come across a snake hibernating for the winter.

Even though the breeze drifting up the gully was cool, perspiration was running down my neck and my legs. I reached into my pocket and found a hair elastic and twisted my now damp hair up into a high ponytail, and let the breeze cool my neck as I turned the last end of the garden bed.

I heard footsteps behind me as I leaned down on the shovel to turn a particularly hard piece of ground. 'Is Mr Sexy Voice here already?' I called out.

There was no answer and I paused. I'd put my foot in it. Resting the shovel against the shed wall I turned slowly just in time to see the glimmer of a smile before his expression went bland.

'Are you expecting more guests for dinner? Or should I be flattered?' My neighbour's voice held a tinge of amusement.

'Oops.' I shrugged and picked up the shovel again. I wasn't terribly concerned about what he thought of me. 'Flattered maybe, but the tag wasn't my creation.'

'No, I didn't for one moment think it would be. Your description would be more "Mr Pain in the Arse", I would imagine.'

Just as well Tam wasn't here to hear him say that, because he even made the word "arse" sound sexy. I lifted my gaze from the hard ground and caught a wide smile on his face. So, he did have a sense of humour after all.

'You pick the name, you take it.' This time the corners of my lips lifted in a brief smile.

There was an awkward silence for a couple of minutes.

'Is dinner ready?' I finally said as I picked up the shovel and put my work boot on it and pressed hard, pleased when the hard soil turned over.

'No, I came out here to have a chat to you. I distinctly got the impression that the dinner invitation was not unanimous.'

I shrugged. I seemed to be doing that a lot lately. 'No skin off my nose. Tam's a great chef, and she was happy to cook a meal for you.'

'If you would prefer me to leave, just say so.'

I went to shrug again, and then forced my shoulders to stay still. I carefully placed the shovel against the wall and folded my arms. 'I'd prefer you to leave, but you're here now, so we might as well have it out.'

He folded his arms. I had to stop thinking of him as "he".

'Okay, what do I call you? Rafe or Jack?"

One eyebrow lifted, and damn if it wasn't as sexy as the voice. It was one of those sardonic lifts that I would love to be able to do. When I lifted my eyebrows for effect, I usually got a laugh from Tam and Nell, and a comment about Groucho Marx eyebrows.

'You know who I am?' The

voice was a bit cooler now, as though somehow, we had breached his privacy.

I suppose we had in one way, but hey, if you were famous, you wore it.

'Yes, we've done our research, and we know who you are or to make it easier for us, we know the *two* people you are. So which one are you?'

To his credit, he looked ill at ease. Maybe embarrassed. He was different to what I had expected from the few brief encounters we'd had.

'Call me Rafe . . . please. . . that is my name.'

'Very well.'

He lifted his hand and pushed back the lock of dark hair that gave him that rakish look. 'And may I call you Pippa?'

'That's my name.'

'I know. Your aunt told me about you.'

My head flew up. This time it was *my* privacy that had been breached. 'Oh? Told you what?'

'She told me she had a niece called Pippa, and that she hoped you'd come back here one day. When the house stayed empty, I wondered if she'd changed her mind about leaving it to you.'

'You seem to know everything then.'

'May we sit down?' He gestured to the small table and chairs that I'd retrieved from the garden shed when I'd mowed the lawn the other day. I was quite proud of how the garden was looking, and I knew this would be a pleasant outdoor area for guests to have breakfast. A pretty native vine with small yellow flowers spilled over the pergola that joined the shed to the back of the house, and the original uneven flagstones edged the lawn. Aunty Vi's birdfeeder hung crookedly from the corner and I made a note to fix it later as we walked across to the table. It was a pretty spot, and I'd spent the last two afternoons out here thinking. I could sense that I was changing; the longer we were on the island, the calmer and more confident I was. I wasn't as anxious as I'd been before, and those constant worries that had dogged me—work and Darren, and the fear that I wasn't good enough—were slowly receding.

Rafe stood until I sat down on the wrought iron chair, and then he sat. I wasn't used to good manners.

Heat filled my cheeks when he put his hands on the table and looked at me. His fingers were pale. Long and elegant. Honestly, with his dark hair and that English skin, he looked like he should be in some period drama, not sitting with me on a tropical island.

I was conscious of my messy hair, stained clothes and dirty hands. I probably smelled too, because I'd found a sealed bag of Dynamic Lifter in the shed and had dug it into the garden.

In contrast, Rafe sat there, spotless in his loose white shirt and a woody fragrance drifted across from him.

I pulled a face and scratched at my neck when a bug landed on it. 'I guess you want to chat about the letter you sent to my solicitor? Maybe it would have been better to make the direct approach than write?'

'I hadn't met you when I wrote it. I'd posted it before you arrived on the island. Yes, I agree, a direct approach is more appropriate now that you are here—and much more polite. That is what I would like to discuss now.' His gaze swept the small garden when he finished talking and I sensed his approval.

'What? Being polite?' I couldn't help myself. I sat straight and spread my hands flat on the table.

'No. Discussing the situation.'

'There is no situation,' I said.

He looked at me now and I held his gaze. A small frisson of something fired and my fingers felt funny. I moved my hands down onto my lap. I wasn't going to get angry or emotional; being able to control my response was an indication of how I'd calmed since we'd arrived.

'You need to accept that I'm not prepared to sell.'

'What if I increased the amount

I'm prepared to offer?'

I shook my head. 'The island is *not* for sale. Not at any price.'

He dropped his head and I noticed his fingers tense on the table, and a glimmer of sympathy ran through me.

I wasn't prepared for the bleak look in his eyes when he finally lifted his head. 'What can I do to get you to understand my reluctance to lose the island?'

'Lose it?'

He waved those elegant fingers again. 'Lose my privacy. That was the reason I came here. Your aunt understood that I needed it.'

'And why does it have to be here?' I was not going to give an inch. 'Surely there are many other places you can have this privacy.'

'Perhaps there are, but I've been here two years now, and I've made myself a home.'

My eyes narrowed. 'Yourself? I wondered if that was your partner you were with the other night?'

His gaze was steely. 'No, that was a business dinner. Not that that is any of your business.'

Ha! The gloves were off.

I smiled and kept it sweet. 'You're right. It's not my business. Equally so, what I intend to do with *my* island is not yours. As far as I can see, the only thing we have to discuss is you handing back the access to Red Wave Wall. In fact, I'd like to see the document that defines the boundary of your land. I can't believe that Aunty Vi would have handed over the access.'

'It's my land, and I'm happy to show you the proof of that.' He gestured around with one hand, and for the life of me I couldn't take my eyes off his fingers. 'Look around you. Do you really want strangers traipsing over this island?'

I held his gaze. His blue eyes were fringed with lashes as dark as his hair.

'You don't have the right to tell me what I can do on this island. Pentecost Island has been accessible to birdwatchers and rock climbers for almost a hundred years, and we are going to build a resort that allows them to stay here in comfort while they explore the island.' I kept my voice hard, but even. I was not going to get emotional.

'And what will that mean for my privacy? Privacy on my land that I bought in good faith, believing that this island would remain the sanctuary that it is,' he said.

'Sanctuary for who? You? Don't you think that's a bit selfish? A whole island just for one.'

'In a word?' His voice was as hard as his eyes. 'No.'

'Well then, like I said before you are going to be very disappointed. Because this resort is going ahead. For the life of me, I can't understand why my aunt sold it to you in the first place.'

'I can tell you why. She had no choice. It was either sell to me or the consortium that was going to buy the whole island. If that had happened, we wouldn't be here having this argument. You would have gotten your inheritance in cold hard cash, and you could have started a resort wherever you wanted. I was the only buyer prepared to take half. I did you a favour.'

'Well it doesn't look like that from where I'm sitting. Are you always used to getting your own way?' I stood and the chair scraped noisily over the flagstones.

'When I am dealing with reasonable people? Yes.' He stood slowly and his chair made no noise as he pushed it beneath the table. 'But I should have anticipated that dealing with a woman would be a waste of time.'

'You dealt with a woman when you bought the place. But I guess that was different because you got your own way then.' I leaned forward at the same time he did, and our noses were almost touching as we glared at each other. The anger coming off him was palpable. His shoulders were stiff, and his mouth was set in a straight line.

'It will be a waste of time this time, because, Mr Rafe Rendell, you will not get your own way. And it has nothing to do with me being a woman. I own this land, and there will be a resort here sooner than you think. If you don't want your precious privacy disturbed, go and buy another island. *You* are the one who's going to have to leave.'

'Well, then I guess. . .' He moved back and I sensed his capitulation was close.

'You guess you accept that there is going to be a resort here?' Triumph ran through me, but his next words were like a bucketful of cold water.

'No, I guess you are going to have to give this project of yours some more consideration. Because I will do everything I can to block your plans.'

By the time I had processed his words, he was heading back towards the house—my house.

And my dining room table.

And now I was expected to sit and be civil across a meal?

His threat had been very real, and I had no doubt he meant every word. And I guessed he had the money to back it. I had the inheritance from Aunty Vi, but I imagined it was nowhere near the amount of money he'd have to fight me.

No way could I sit at dinner and pretend everything was hunky dory now that we'd both said our piece. I picked up the shovel and pushed it into the ground, satisfied when the hard earth yielded at my first push. I muttered beneath my breath as I finished turning the soil in the last garden bed. I was looking forward to getting some plants in and watching the garden regenerate.

I was looking forward to seeing the house renovated and the resort huts and restaurant go up along the foreshore.

I was going to regenerate here too. I was not going to let Rafe Rendell get beneath my skin. I needed to get my head and heart in sync. I was not going back to dinner because he would be in my house, being waited on and mooned over by my two supposed friends.

I pulled my phone out. Stuff staying here. I'd take the launch over to Hamilton Island and catch up with Evie. Tam and Nell could entertain our famous neighbour to their heart's content.

Evie picked up on the first ring.

'Evie, It's Pippa Carmichael.'

'Hey, Pip. I was going to call you tomorrow. I've got some spare time and I was going to sail over and visit you.'

'I was hoping to come over to

Hamo and see you tonight. Do you have plans?'

'Damn, not tonight. I'm over on the mainland. I don't come back across the Passage until tomorrow. But I was going to come straight to Pentecost Island if it suited you and catch up with the three of you. It's been ages since we were all together. I found a photo on my phone the other day after I bumped into Tam and Nell. The four of us sitting on a beach when we were on a uni break. They were good times.'

'That was a great holiday. Look, Evie, come over tomorrow. I've got some work coming up I'd like to discuss with you.'

'Sounds great. I'll leave here early, so I'll be there mid-morning.'

'Sailing across, you said?'

'Yep, I've fallen in love with this place, and I bought myself a boat. She's rough, but good enough to live on and get me across to Airlie Beach where I've been getting most of my work. I've had a three-month contract over there working on the new foreshore development, but I finished up this week.'

'Perfect timing then,' I said. 'Can't wait to catch up tomorrow.'

Chapter 18
Tam

'Thank you for inviting me, anyway.'

Stunned, Tam stared at Nell as Rafe closed the door behind him quietly. He'd made his apologies and said he wouldn't be staying for dinner after all. He'd been polite, but his words had been clipped and brief, and his body language screamed stress.

Big time.

'What the heck did she say now?' Nell spluttered. 'I thought you said Pip had mellowed a bit towards him?'

Tam shook her head. 'She wasn't happy about him coming over, but she was going to talk to him.'

'Well, she obviously has. Did you see how upset he looked? I feel sorry for the poor man.'

Tam crossed to the gas stove and lowered the flame beneath the stir fry that she was keeping warm. 'Yeah, me too. But there's something there that doesn't jell for me.' She reached for the rice packet. 'We might as well eat now. I wonder where Pip is.'

'What do you mean by doesn't jell?' Nell stood by the table as Tam poured rice into the saucepan of boiling water.

'You found him on the internet. He's from England. He's obviously rich and famous, so why is he holed up here on a small island off the east coast of Australia, protecting his privacy at all costs? There must be a story behind it. Something's not right.'

Nell looked thoughtful. 'Maybe. There were no recent articles about him, and it's been a couple of years since his last book came out.'

'And he's here by himself. My curiosity is at "Danger, Will Robinson level."'

'You could be right. But Pip still needs to tone down. She's obviously upset him. That's not the way to deal on a business level. She has to learn to hold her emotions in. I'm going to have a talk to her.'

Tam flicked a glance at Nell and worry churned in her stomach. 'Maybe it's better to give her some space. I've been worried about her since we arrived. Even though this is what she wants, I think she's a bit fragile.'

'Do you think so? I haven't got that impression at all.'

'Pip's always been a master at covering up her feelings and pretending she's okay. I know coming back here was hard for her.

She's carrying a lot of guilt about not coming up to visit her aunt before she died. Remember how much she changed when she was living up here? It was the first time in her life she'd felt loved. And she was confident enough to tell us how she felt about it when she came down to uni. And now Aunty Vi has gone and she's alone again.'

'She's got us. And she seems content to me.' Nell frowned as Tam crossed over to the sink.

'Yes, she has. But we also have our own families, and we're all Pip has.' Tam picked up the dishcloth and started wiping down the benchtops. 'I just remember what happens when she has a setback. In the past few weeks she's broken up with Darren, lost the job that she put her heart and soul into, come back to an island where her aunt isn't anymore, and now the only positive— her dream of this resort—is being threatened. I'm sorry I asked Rafe over for dinner. I'll go and find her and see if she's okay.'

Nell shook her head. 'No, I'll go. You pair will end up fighting.'

'True. And that's the last thing she needs. Tell her to come in and have dinner. It's almost ready. The rice will be about another five minutes.' Tam stood at the window staring out over the small garden.

Chapter 19

Rafe

I sat on the balcony overlooking the sea and nursed my second whisky. The first one had gone down fast, and the mellow burn had gone a small way to easing my anger and frustration. I focused on breathing in and out as the sun sank behind the hills of the mainland.

The colours in the sky behind the sinking orange orb made my fingers tingle as words filled my thoughts. Vermillion, indigo, gold and pale apricot vied for supremacy as the sun slipped below the hills. Gradually my body relaxed and the sound of the gentle wind sighing in the rainforest below helped me calm.

No matter how much I tried to justify why I must have the whole island, I knew I was being unreasonable. My portion was less than half of the whole island, and if I was honest, I had always known the situation would change when Ma Carmichael passed away.

When I'd asked her real name when we'd first met on the wharf that had been at their end of the bay before the cyclone, she'd laughed. Ma had been a big woman, larger than life, and it was hard to imagine her outgoing personality being confined in an aged care facility.

'It's Violet, but don't you dare call me that. I've been Ma to everyone who matters to me for many years.'

I'd been honoured to join that group of people she considered friends, and if I didn't go over to her house with the whisky bottle late in the afternoon, I'd see her making her way slowly up the track to my new house on sunset. Apart from the staff at the general provisions store on Hamilton Island, Ma Carmichael was the only other person I had communicated with for the first two months I lived on the island, until she left to live on the mainland.

I'll never forget that day. I went down to the wharf to say goodbye and the look in Ma's eyes broke my heart. She knew she'd never be coming back to the island, and I'd gripped her hand as I helped her onto the launch. It made me think more about my situation, and I vowed that I could be strong as Ma had been. But I'd backslid and wallowed in my misery.

Jenny emailed me constantly, and I would occasionally reply, but the conversations with Ma had kept me sane. She asked no questions, but I had found myself telling my story. She wasn't one to comment or show sympathy, but one night she'd looked at me over her whisky tumbler.

'A story shared is a way to start healing, but I think you have a way to go yet.'

That's all she'd said, and I appreciated her respecting my privacy, although a person would have had to be blind not to see how depressed I was.

I wouldn't even admit it to myself.

The problem was now that every time I looked at Pippa, I could see in her eyes that same love for the island, and I didn't want to see that same sadness that I had witnessed in Ma's eyes if I blocked her development.

I had no doubt I could take

legal action and block it for years. In the end, it would go ahead, but it would stuff up her plans in the interim.

You'd think on an island miles from civilisation I could be satisfied with things whatever happened. What was a few people wandering around looking at birds and climbing rocks?

I picked up the bottle and went to pour a third glass, but I hesitated.

Ah what the hell. I only half filled the glass and lifted it to the sky.

'For you, Ma Carmichael. I can only hope you're not looking down and seeing me stuff things up.'

I was ashamed of myself. I'd gone hard on Pippa this afternoon. I'd hoped that she had come to the island on a whim, and that she wouldn't stay, but too late, I was coming to realise that I had gone in too hard.

Way too hard.

At least I hadn't let slip that Ma had spent a lot of time talking about her great-niece and how proud she was of her. She'd told me of the years that Pippa had lived on the island, and how those years had turned her around, and she'd developed confidence as she'd completed high school.

'She had a lonely childhood,' Ma had said. 'My sister's daughter—Pippa's mother—was a strange woman.'

But she hadn't ever said what was strange about her. Apparently, there'd been a tragedy that had resulted in Pippa living with Ma, but she'd never given any details, despite my curiosity.

Real lives were always fodder for an author. Even one who was having trouble writing these days, but curiosity had tugged at me.

All I knew was that Ma was the only family that Pippa had, and she'd worried how she'd cope when she was left alone.

'When she came to me, she was damaged, and I'd hate to see her go back to that. She didn't utter one word for the first six weeks after I took her in.'

I looked up at the sky and held the glass aloft again. 'I don't think you have anything to worry about, Ma. She's a confident woman now and she knows what she wants.'

Putting the glass on the small table beside my chair, I leaned back and enjoyed the darkness. I always felt cocooned once the sun had gone. In the tropics the dark was instant; occasionally I longed for the softness of an English twilight.

Pippa Carmichael and I were going to have to come to a compromise. I knew I was going to have to give a little. I wasn't going to leave, and I knew now that Pippa and her friends had the same intention. Their friendship seemed tight, and I wondered why they had come with her. Surely the three women didn't think they were going to singlehandedly develop a resort from that old house and overgrown block of ground.

'Sexist, Jack.' The voice from my past drilled into my thoughts, disturbing the peace of my thoughts flitting around in the growing dark. 'Sexist, selfish and totally self-absorbed,' she'd said.

I'd glanced at Rebecca, not realising it was the last fight we'd ever have. To me, this one was no different from the many arguments that had been a feature of our five-year marriage. One of the biggest ones had been about her insistence to call me by my pen name.

Rebecca hadn't stopped despite the disinterested gaze I threw her way. 'You know, I think I preferred it when you were toddling off to work at that shitty little accountant's office in the village.'

I hadn't been able to help myself. 'And you preferred living in that dark little cottage?'

She'd stared at me and then turned to look at the Thames. When my second book had taken off, we'd moved to London, to a luxury apartment at Dockside.

'No, you know I love living here, but really, Jack? What's the point in living in the city when you sit hunched up at that computer all day?'

'Perhaps to make the money

that you enjoy spending?' I hadn't been able to help myself and her glare had been icy.

'We are expected at Mummy and Daddy's this weekend. There is a house party and everyone who is everyone will be there.'

'So, we are everyone too?' I'd raised my eyebrows at that ludicrous description. 'I have a deadline, even if they are expecting Jack Smith to be there.'

'Jesus, Jack. Surely you can take two days off.'

That particular weekend I had a deadline for galley proofs. The proofs of *The Legacy*, my last successful novel. I'd stood and crossed to the window and put my arms around her. 'I'm sorry, sweetheart. You go, and I'll try to come up on Sunday.'

'No, you choose. Your book or me! I told Mummy we would be

there tonight. Both of us.'

'I'll get the train on Sunday.'
I'd leaned across and brushed my lips across her cheek, but Rebecca had turned her head away.

'Don't bother,' she'd snapped. Half an hour later, when she slammed the door on her way out, it was the last time I saw my wife.

The residual bitterness had drilled a huge hole in my self-confidence and my ability to write, and it had been luck that the movie deals had come through in the months following that weekend. I had a guaranteed income and moved as far away as I could.

I'd had an accountant friend who had emigrated and lived in Cairns, and he invited me over to visit.

Since Jenny had come over to see where the next book was at, I knew I had to lift myself out of this bitter self-pity and start writing again. I had wasted enough of my life.

But before then, I had to find Pippa Carmichael and tell her I was willing to compromise.

Tomorrow was a new day.

Compromise was something I was not good at. If I had been, I would still be married and living in the UK.

As the night settled around me, I drew a deep breath, determined to keep the usual darkness from my soul. I stood and made my way inside. I would find something to eat, and then I would find some new words from within.

I glanced at the clock in the living room on my way to the kitchen. There was a frozen quiche in the deep freezer, and I allowed myself a regretful grin. If I'd taken more care tonight, I could have been over at my neighbours' house where a tantalising smell had drifted from the kitchen.

As I opened the freezer, a loud knocking stopped me in my tracks. Not one person had knocked at the front door of this house since I'd moved in over two years ago. Ma had wandered over and settled herself on the balcony when she had visited, waiting until I came out with two glasses.

Tam and Nell stood on my doorstep and I frowned, automatically looking past them for Pippa.

They were alone.

Before I could ask them why they were at my house at nine-thirty at night, Nell grabbed my arm.

'We need your help, Rafe. Please.'

Concern surged through me

when I saw the worry on Nell's face, and Tam's rigid stance. 'Where's Pippa?' I asked.

'We don't know. We can't find her.'

'Find her? What do you mean?' My frown deepened as I looked from one to the other. Tam ran a shaking hand through her untidy curls.

'She didn't come in for dinner, and now we don't know where she is.'

Nell interrupted. 'I went outside to get her, and we had words. I marched inside, and Tam and I ate dinner without her. Pippa was in one of her moods. When it got late, we went outside and called her, but we couldn't find her. She's nowhere in the house, or in the garden or down at the beach. We've been looking for more than an hour now.'

'Pippa has had some issues lately, and we're a bit worried about her. She was in a bit of a state when Nell spoke to her.' Tam held my gaze steadily.

'What are you saying?' A cold pit of dread opened in my stomach. If she was in a state, I had contributed to it.

'Pippa's mother committed suicide when Pippa was twelve, and when she's down, she often wonders if she's inherited her mother's instability.' Tam's eyes were bleak. 'We've always supported her, and brought her up when things got her down, but she's never taken off before. I'm worried. This move to the island has been a big thing for her. For all of us.'

'Shit.' The cold in my stomach spread to my limbs. 'Where have you looked? What do you need me to do? Where can I search?'

Chapter 20
Rafe

Two hours later, I'd twice walked the track where I'd passed Pippa on my morning walks. I walked from the bottom to the middle of the hill calling her name until I was hoarse. Tam and Nell were looking along the foreshore in our bay—funny how suddenly I'd accepted their right to be here and now thought of it as *our* bay—and now they'd gone back to the house to see if Pippa had come home while they'd been out searching. Both times when I reached the halfway point on the hill where we'd had a conversation, I'd been tempted to climb higher. It was hard to pinpoint why, but I had a feeling I should keep going. The second time I stopped at the false crest of the hill halfway up and looked ahead. The moon had risen, and the wind had dropped. The side of the island and the mountain ahead were bathed in bright light.

I cocked my head to the side and listened; for an instant I thought I'd heard a cry. As I stood waiting for the sound again, a bird dipped below the side of the hill and let out a mournful cry.

False alarm.

I knew the island well. I'd taken many walks in the two years that I'd lived here, and I wondered if maybe she'd gone to Red Wave Wall, where the rock climbers went. The cold in the pit of my stomach spread again as I thought of the high wall that rose over the sea.

I turned and pulled out my phone. I had exchanged numbers with Tam before I set off, and I pressed the speed dial I'd set.

'Any luck?' I asked as soon as she answered.

'No, not a sign of her. You?'

'No, nothing, but I've decided to go up to Red Wave Wall.' My breath hitched, I'd continued striding up the hill as I'd called, without making a conscious decision to go up.

'Be careful. From memory, the path out there is a bit dicey, and it won't be easy in the dark.' What she didn't voice was what we both thinking: the sheer cliff with the huge drop down to the water.

'I will. I've been there a few times, so I know it well. I'll call you if I—'

Tam cut me off, and I could hear the tears in her voice. 'Thank you. We'll wait for your call. Just go. We'll keep looking in the rainforest.'

For a while the only sound was

my heavy breathing, and the blood pulsing in my ears. Occasionally there was a rustle in the undergrowth on the side of the path, and the flapping of wings at the edge of the cliff. The higher I got, the narrower the path got, and I was grateful for the bright moonlight. I paused to catch my breath and looked to the east. A bright swathe of moonlight illuminated the sea and it glowed silver all the way to the horizon.

It was a beautiful sight, and I wished I'd taken more time to appreciate the beauty of this island. I reached the fork in the track and closed my eyes as I decided whether to go to Red Wave Wall or the peak of the mountain.

I let instinct guide me and took the left fork to Red Wave Wall, the escarpment that was a popular rock-climbing destination. The occasional climbers hadn't bothered me as they didn't come over to my side of the island. Sometimes I'd seen boats moored over there, but no one had come to my bay. The track petered out and I hugged the cliff wall. No sound disturbed my concentration as I negotiated the narrowest part of the way to the top.

I realised that I'd been quiet too, and I hadn't called out for of the past couple of hundred metres.

'Pippa! Pippa! Can you hear me?'

A flock of parrots rose squawking from a tree about fifty metres ahead of me and I jumped. At the same time, loud footsteps thudded on the top of the escarpment above me, and I looked up as a shower of rocks and stones tumbled down to the track ahead.

'Pippa?' I called loudly. 'Is that you? Are you all right?'

The only answer was a long drawn out bleating from above.

I knew there were wild goats on the island, but I'd only encountered them once before. That time they'd taken off when I'd walked towards them, and I hadn't been too concerned, despite Ma's warning that the males could be dangerous if they felt their herd was under threat.

I swallowed as I looked at the huge drop on my left. I certainly didn't want to meet an angry goat on this track. Lowering my head so I could watch where I was placing my feet, I picked up my pace and expelled a relieved breath when I reached the top of the wall. The eastern side of the crest was clear and there was no sign of anyone there—Pippa or goats. I turned and as I made my way into the rainforest that covered the western half of the peak, I thought I heard something.

'I paused and waited. 'Pippa!' I called again.

'Hello?' The voice was soft and tentative.

'Pippa?' I took off into the forest, no longer worried about encountering a goat.

'I'm here.'

I stopped and spun around. This time her voice was behind me. In my hurry to set off I stupidly hadn't thought of bringing a torch. I dug in my pocket and pulled out my phone and turned the flashlight on. I swung it in a wide arc from the cliff face to the forest, but there was no one there.

'Where are you?'

'I'm here. Above you.'

I looked up as I realised that

her voice was coming from the tree. I shone the light up into the thick foliage. 'I can't see you.'

'I can see you down there. I'm higher.'

I stepped back and craned my head and lifted the phone, but the light didn't light up more than the first five metres of the trunk and branches.

'Have I got the right tree?'

'Yes. I climbed higher because the branches were thicker up here, and I felt safer.'

Sweet relief flooded through me. 'Stay there. Don't move.'

'And where do you think I'm going to go?' Her voice was dry.

'Are you hurt?'

'Only my pride.'

'Just wait.' I hit speed dial and Tam answered immediately.

'Rafe?' Hesitancy laced her voice and I rushed to reassure her.

'All's well. I've found her. Pippa's fine.'

'Where are you? We'll come.'

'No stay there. We're up at Red Wave Wall. I'll bring her back down. See you in a while." I disconnected and stood at the base of the tree.

'Are you going to come down?' I didn't dare ask why she was up a tree on the highest point of the island in the middle of the night.

'I would if I could. I'm stuck.'

'Are you all right though?' Even though I was a wordsmith, I didn't know how to put it into words, how to ask her if she was *really* okay. I needed that reassurance from her.

'Yes, I'm fine. I just can't get down.'

'Ah, may I ask what you were doing up there in the first place?'

'I was running away from the biggest, meanest goat I have ever seen.'

'A goat?'

'Yes, a goat. He put his head down and went for me. His horns were huge, and I had visions of ending up over the cliff if he caught me.'

You weren't the only one who was thinking that, I thought, but I didn't say anything.

'Why can't you get down?' I peered up but I still couldn't see how high she was.

'I didn't look when I was climbing up, but now there's a huge gap down to the next branch, and I'm not game to go down in case I slip.'

I moved closer to the tree and looked up, but I still couldn't see her. 'How far up do you think you are?'

'About eight metres, I'd say.'

'Bloody hell, that is high. What

do you want me to do? It's a bit far to go and get a ladder.'

This time her voice held a note of fear. 'No! Don't go. Stay there, please.'

'I won't leave you.'

'I thought I was going to have to stay here until daybreak. I was scared I'd nod off and fall, but if you stay there and talk to me, it'll help me stay awake.'

'And I'm probably the last person you really want to talk to, so I'll make the most of it.'

'Probably,' she said, and her voice didn't sound too shaky.

I reached up and grabbed the branch that was just below my shoulder height and swung myself up. 'I'm coming up.'

'Be careful.'

'I'll have you know I'm a very experienced tree climber.'

'Oh? Why's that? I can't

imagine you being an outdoors person.'

'I'm deeply hurt,' I said. 'You've seen me out walking, how many times?'

'Three.' The reply came quickly. 'But that's not an outdoorsy thing.'

'I grew up in the country and I even had my own treehouse.'

'Lucky you.'

Too late, I remembered her sad childhood and I cursed myself silently. 'Did you ever read the *Magic Faraway Tree*?' I looked up as I reached for the third branch and caught a glimpse of a red sneaker through the leaves.

'Yes, I did. And it's funny that you mention it because I was thinking about it while I was trying to figure out how to fill in the hours. I loved that story. I have a copy back at the house.'

As I hauled myself up to the next branch, there was a gap in the foliage and I could see two red sneakers now, dangling either side of a thick branch about two metres above me. If I could get up there, I could help Pip back down.

'I can see you.' One hand slipped as I looked up and I reached for the trunk with the other. My fingers touched something cold and smooth and I pulled my hand back. 'Holy mother of God, there's a fucking snake here.'

'What colour is it? Pippa's voice was calm.

'Jesus, I don't know.' I peered down to where it had slithered past my hand. 'Green, I think.'

'Yeah, same one I saw on the way up. It's only a tree snake. Harmless. It won't bite you.'

My hands were shaking now,

and I found it difficult to get a grip.

A grip on the branch, and on my equilibrium.

'I'd rather face a goat than a snake. I hate them. I'm a Pom, remember.'

'Don't be a sook. I told you it's harmless.'

I swallowed and reached for the next branch and pulled myself up. This time the branch below was wide enough to put my feet on. 'I'm not a sook. I'm coming to rescue you.'

I was encouraged by the chuckle from above. I looked up, and this time my gaze encountered a pair of green eyes staring down at me.

'Hello,' I said.

'If you were not going to be my rescuer, I probably wouldn't talk to you.' She was straddling a solid branch, leaning against a part of the trunk that had a wide curved section recessed into the timber. I felt reassured. She looked quite safe there.

'I don't blame you. I'm actually quite pleased that we've met tonight.'

'Oh? That surprises me.'

'Can you move your legs a bit closer to the trunk and I'll come up to your branch.'

I waited as she lifted her legs and tucked them against her chest. I paused when I heard Pippa drag in a deep shuddering breath.

'I don't feel as safe with my legs up.'

I tried to inject a soothing tone into my voice. 'You look very safe where you are. You're in a bit of an alcove.'

Reaching up I swung myself up to the branch that she was on. As I did, I made the mistake of looking down. The moonlight illuminated the ground below and my stomach lurched. I froze.

Bloody hell. Had I climbed up that far? No wonder Pippa didn't want to risk climbing down.

'How the blazes did you get this high?'

She must have seen the expression on my face as I hung on for grim death.

'It's okay. Hang on tight, and crawl over here. The branch is wide enough and there's room for two against the trunk.'

I took a deep breath and held her gaze in the filtered moonlight as I inched along the branch towards her.

Chapter 21

Pippa

The last thing I'd expected when I'd strode up towards Red Wave Wall as the sun set was to spend the night stuck in a tree with my nemesis. After Rafe had crawled along the branch, we sat shoulder to shoulder with our legs just touching. Although to be honest, since he'd climbed up to rescue me, being rude and ungrateful was out of the question. Anyway, I'd walked off my temper—and my hurt with Nell—as I'd climbed the hill.

Nell's words had been totally out of character. They had been blunt, and I'd shut down and walked away.

'It's time to grow up, Pip, and think of others,' she'd thrown at me as I'd walked towards the path.

The truth often hurts the most, though, doesn't it?

The spectacular sunset over the mainland had soothed my soul, and I'd sent a quick thank you up to Aunty Vi. As serenity took over and I eased my walking pace, I thought about what I'd do. No matter what happened with Rafe Rendell, I intended staying on the island. Surely we could come to some sort of agreement. Once I got council approval, there was no legal reason why I couldn't go ahead with my plan. In fact, the response from the tourism body had been really positive. I'd decided to meet with him again and try to come to a compromise. Without any emotion involved.

I shifted awkwardly as I sat next to him. There had been an uncomfortable silence since he'd moved across next to me.

'Careful,' he said. 'I wanted to—'

'Wait. Before you say anything about getting down from here, I want to apologise to you for the way I spoke to you in the garden. I was rude and out of line.'

He turned his head and looked at me. I couldn't see his eyes because the light was behind him, but his words were sincere. 'You beat me to it. I wasn't going to talk about getting you out of this tree. I was going to apologise to you. I was sitting on my balcony watching the sunset, and I came to the same conclusion. The way I spoke to you was unforgivable, especially the bit about dealing with a woman. I'm very sorry.'

'Good.' I put my head down as he continued to stare at me. 'I'll accept your apology if you accept mine, and we can try to work together.'

His voice was quiet. 'I accept that you have a right to build your resort. I won't do anything to block it.'

'Really? You mean that? As I looked down, the huge drop to the ground made me shiver.

'It's okay. Please don't be scared. I won't let you fall.' Rafe reached down and took my hand in his and looked down at my fingers. 'And yes, I mean it.'

'We've still got to get down,' I said shakily.

'Let's talk and take your mind off it. When it's light it will seem a lot easier.'

'You think so?' I stared down at my hand in his. 'Okay, talk to me.'

'You've been working hard on your project already, and I know it means a lot to you. I couldn't believe what you've done to the house and garden in what . . . less than a week?' His fingers were smooth against mine as I nodded, and a wave of embarrassment rose in my chest. My fingers were dirt-stained and rough from working outside.

I swallowed as heat rushed to my cheeks. 'Yes. And it does mean a lot to me. It's where I want to stay. Tam and Nell are here to get me started, and another friend is coming over tomorrow. I have a feeling she'll stay for a while too. Resort or not, it is where I am going to spend the rest of my life.' I lifted my head. 'For the past little while, I've not been happy, but I know now that I've come home. This is the place where I want to be.'

'We're a fine pair.' He let go of my hand and my fingers were cool. 'I guess I could say the same. I've been finding my way since I came to the island, and it's taken a while to decide where I want to be, but I don't want to go back to what was my home.'

'In England? I asked.

He nodded.

'Why did you come here? Why did you buy half of the island?'

'Do you believe in serendipity, Pippa?'

'In what context? Finding something without looking?'

'Yes, some would say it's good luck when you unintentionally stumble across something good, but I think it goes deeper than that. I was meant to meet Ma on the mainland. She was over there for the first time for a long time, she told me. She was looking at the aged care home.'

'Where did you meet her?"

'Would you believe in a bottle

shop in the whisky section?'

A grin tugged at my lips. 'I would. Aunty Vi was an expert. It was her Scottish heritage.'

'She gave me some advice, and we got talking. Before I knew it we were in the local hotel. The deal was sealed that night.'

'She would have still been here when your house was built?' I asked.

'Yes, for a few months. We spent many nights talking. She was a good woman.'

'She was. She certainly made a difference to my life.'

Rafe turned to look at me. 'I believe I was meant to meet her, and I believe I was meant to live on the island. That's why my reaction to your resort was over the top. But I've had time to think about it. So long as I can retain my privacy, I think we can work together.'

'Your privacy?' A rogue grin pulled at my lips. 'I was thinking of having meet-the-author drinks, and afternoon teas where you could talk about your books. You know? Make it a feature of the resort.'

He stiffened beside me and his voice was horrified. 'What!'

I chuckled. 'I'm sorry. I couldn't help it. Of course I wouldn't do that. We won't bother you.'

'Witch,' he said, but his voice was warm. 'Not a kind way to treat your rescuer.'

'I haven't seen any rescuing happening yet.' I nudged him.

'Yes, it is rather problematic. I'm not terribly keen to go down past that snake.'

'And I'm not *terribly keen* to climb down in the dark.' I parrotted his words and accent.

'Are you trying to be smart?' he said.

'Not at all. What if that big buck goat is still down there?'

'There were goats above the track as I got to the top of the hill.'

'That settles it. I'm not going down there in the dark.' I folded my arms.

'So you propose that we stay in the tree all night?'

I nodded. 'I'd already decided that before you arrived. Like I said before, I was scared of going to sleep. I put in a big day, and I'm tired. I was worried I'd fall.'

'I'll ring Tam and tell her that we are going to stay up on the hill for the night. There's no need to worry her and tell her that we're stuck up a tree.'

'Did Tam come and ask you to look for me? I thought they might be worried when I didn't front.'

'Tam and Nell both came knocking on my door.'

'Oh shit. I suppose they thought the worst.'

'They were very worried. They'd been looking everywhere for you.'

'My phone is back at the house.'

Rafe leaned back and pulled his phone from his pocket and pressed a button. 'Tam? We've decided it's a bit dark to come down safely—he shot me a look and I smiled back—' so we'll see you in the morning.'

I nudged him again. 'Tell Tam I said to say sorry to Nell for me. And I'm sorry for taking off and worrying them.'

He did as I asked and then disconnected.

'What did Tam say?' I asked.

'You really want to hear?' He

put the phone back in his shirt pocket. 'She said you're going to be very, very sorry. I wouldn't rush back.'

'I guess I'm in trouble then.'

'I guess you are.' Then a serious note. 'You're very lucky to have good friends who care about you.'

'Yep. We're tight.' I ventured a question. 'Tell me if I'm out of line, but what about you? Don't you get lonely here by yourself?'

'I enjoy my own company.' His words were clipped.

'Fair enough.'

There was silence for a while, and then Rafe broke it. 'I was married for five years. When that ended, I decided that I'd be happier alone.'

'Well, you are certainly alone here. A bit drastic maybe, to move to a deserted island to find solitude.'

'Perhaps.' Silence again. 'I thought Rebecca was the love of my life. I'd known her since school, and I adored her. All I wanted was to make her happy. But I wasn't good enough for her. She resented me spending so much of my time writing.'

'Didn't she know that before she married you?'

'No. I was an accountant when we were married. My first book was accepted a couple of years after that.'

'But wasn't she happy for you?' This time I couldn't hold my curiosity in.

'Not really. It only took me a couple of years of marriage to realise that my feelings weren't really reciprocated as I thought. I came from a wealthy background, plus I was on a good salary when we were married. And then when the first book deal came through, so did the money . . .' His bitterness was obvious.

'I thought that was your wife that night last week, when you were in the restaurant. She didn't look very happy.'

'That was Jenny, my publisher's wife. And no, she wasn't happy. You see the problem is—and I haven't told anyone else this—is that the dream of being here and writing didn't eventuate. I've spent a lot of time feeling sorry for myself. Jenny was here to chase my next book up.'

'And?'

'I received an email and in a very short time I decided to take myself off, find somewhere new to live, and devote myself to my writing. And it's strange but these last few days I've had some success.

'Email? What sort of email would make you do that?'

'My marriage was ended by a single email. Rebecca had gone to her parents for the weekend. I was supposed to go on the Sunday, but she emailed me before I left to tell me not to bother as the marriage was over. I haven't seen her since that afternoon she left. The settlement and divorce were all done without meeting again.'

'Sorry, but you're probably better off without someone who could do that.' He looked sad and I felt sorry for him. Rafe was talking to me to stop me being scared, and he'd opened up to me. Now it was my turn.

'You want to hear something to top your email story?'

'Can you?'

'I can. I wish *my* partner had

broken it off by email. Then I would have been spared the indignity of seeing his floozy in my bathroom in a pink G string.'

He snorted, and I wasn't sure if it was a laugh he was trying to cover up or if I'd shocked his very proper English sensibilities.

'Sorry,' he murmured. 'And yes, that would have been most upsetting, I imagine. Why was she in your bathroom? Sorry, that might be a bit personal. I'll take that back.'

'Not at all. I was in the bath and he thought I was at work, so he brought her home for a romp in our bed.' I yawned. 'Anyway, it was all for the best. I saw for myself what Tam and Nell had been trying to tell me for months.' I covered my mouth as I fought another yawn. 'And look where we ended up. A happy outcome all around.'

'If you'd like to put your head on my shoulder, I'll make sure you don't slip if you'd like to have some sleep. It will make the time go faster.'

Reluctance fought my tiredness. 'That's very kind, but . . .' God, I was starting to get an English accent. I must be tired.

'No buts.' Rafe lifted his arm and I paused and then moved closer and rested my head on his shoulder. His white shirt smelled fresh like linen, and I could feel the warmth of his skin through the fabric.

'Promise you won't let me fall,' I murmured.

'I promise.'

***

Rafe

I kept my promise that night and had been surprised when Pippa had slept against me until the first rays of sunlight broke through the leaves of the tree where we'd spent the night. The climb down had been much easier than we'd anticipated, and she'd appeared slightly sheepish.

We'd not encountered a snake or a goat on our journey home.

I will be forever grateful that I had discovered her in the tree that night, but that story will come later. Something had shifted between us and even though we had only had a week's acquaintance—most of it acrimonious—we forged a solid friendship in those few hours in the branches of that tree.

I walked her back to the house, where Tam and Nell were waiting on the front porch. Emotion clogged my throat as Pippa left my side and ran into their open arms.

'I know what you would have thought, you pair of dills. I promised you that I would never give you any cause for worry. I was just upset, and I didn't realise how late it was.'

Tam went to say something and shook her head. I was surprised to see tears in her eyes. Nell spoke for her. 'Don't you ever, ever worry us like that again, young lady.'

'Yes, mother hen.' Pippa chuckled. 'Everything is good now.'

Tam and Nell's eyes widened when she came back to me and linked her arm through mine. 'This good man found me and looked after me until it was light enough to . . . um . . . walk back down from Red Wave Wall. Thank you, Rafe.' She reached up and brushed her lips across my cheek, and something shifted irrevocably inside me. I've always scoffed at love at first sight stories, or those who said they knew when they had met their soul mate. Maybe it was on fifth sight, but I knew that Pippa Carmichael was a woman I wanted to get to know a lot better.

'My pleasure. It's time I was heading home.'

'Can we at least give you breakfast? Tam scrambles a mean egg.' Pippa's fingers rested on my arm and my nerve endings fired.

I was torn. I didn't want to leave, but I was keen to go back to my house and sit at the computer. As Pippa had rested against me last night, and I'd felt her breath puff on my neck, I had been filled with inspiration. I had plotted most of a story as the night had passed. I wanted to get it down before it left me. 'I'll come over later today and have a coffee with you. Would that be suitable?'

As I turned to go, Pippa gasped.

'Oh my God. No!'

I turned with a frown, but she wasn't looking at me. Her mouth was open and she was pointing at a small yacht that was sailing into the bay. The bright pink headsail was full of the south-easterly wind and the boat was coming in fast. As we watched the motor kicked in and the pink sail dropped into the sail bag. A woman stood at the helm and waved madly as she came closer to the wharf.

'It's Evie,' Tam cried.

'Is it okay if she goes onto your wharf?' Nell asked me.

'Of course.' I saw the look that Nell and Tam exchanged.

I turned to Pippa. Her brow was wrinkled in a frown and her hands were on her hips. 'What's the matter?'

'A bloody pink sail,' she said dejectedly.

'It's all right,' Tam said. 'It's down now. I'm sure she's got a white one.'

'All right. I guess I can live with that. See you later, Rafe.'

'You will.' I nodded and stood there bemused as the trio made their way down the path and towards my wharf.

Finally, I made my way back to the hill and ignored the call of both coffee and a shower. I sat at my desk and the words flowed from my fingers.

Chapter 22

A month later
Pippa

Evie had kept the pink sail in the sail bag and had moved into the house with us. Her yacht, *Eros*, was moored around at Back Bay because our shared jetty wasn't big enough for three boats. She'd jumped at the opportunity of working with us, and the past month had flown by in a flurry of positives. One more added to the payroll, but it was worth it.

I was on top of the world and often found myself smiling for no real reason. It was the happiest I had been for a long time, and every day affirmed that my decision to come to Pentecost Island had been the right one.

With the backing of the tourism board, the development approval had flown through the local council. Our furniture had come across from the mainland on the barge and we'd hired a boat to bring it over from Hamo. The floors had been stripped and sanded, and the inside of the house had been painted throughout.

It was amazing how much work five people could achieve in a day.

Yes, five people.

Rafe was a constant and *welcome* visitor. That is, on the day or two or three a week he took off from his writing. But if he didn't come over for the day, he would come over for dinner.

I feared it was Tam's cooking that brought him over.

I'd seen the looks that Tam sent our way when we were head-to-head talking, but Rafe was simply telling me of the progress he was making with his book.

One evening about a week ago, Tam had called me into the kitchen while she was cooking dinner. Nell was immersed adding expenses to the accounts spreadsheet—the bills were beginning to come in—at the desk that we'd set up in the alcove off the dining room. It would eventually be the reception area and we were planning to build a wall to close it off from the back of the house. We needed a carpenter and were thinking of advertising to see if we could entice someone to come to the island for a few months. Many of the building jobs were too big for us to take on; we simply didn't have the expertise, and we had to build to cyclone specifications Evie was out on the track checking the solar lights that she'd installed that afternoon.

'What's up?' I said as I lifted

the lid of the pot that was bubbling on the stove. 'Yum, spaghetti bolognaise. Are we having garlic bread too? I'm starving.'

Tam leaned back against the sink and regarded me steadily. 'I just wanted to check you're going okay, Pip.'

I turned and widened my eyes. 'Okay? I've never been better. Why?'

'It wouldn't have anything to do with our sexy Englishman, would it? You've been different since that night you spent up on the mountain with him.'

Up the tree, I thought, but I didn't say anything.

Rafe and I had never shared our secret about spending the night in the tree. Not for any particular reason, and we hadn't talked about not mentioning it. I think it was because it had been such a special night for both of us.

For me, at least, it had been a turning point in my life.

I shook my head. 'Rafe and I are simply good friends.'

'I don't want to see you hurt again, Pip. And I don't want it to get to a situation where it might be difficult to be on the island with him. I mean if you did get together and then break up.'

I was hurt, but then I realised that Tam was only concerned about me. 'My track record of breakups is only because I was shit at picking a decent guy.'

'I won't disagree with that,' she said.

I turned the tables on her. 'You think Rafe is from the same mould as Darren and the other jerks I hooked up with?'

'Hell, no. He's a gentleman.'

'So, what's the problem?'

Her expression was mutinous. 'We're just keeping an eye out for you.'

I walked over and held my arms open. 'Come here.'

Tam came over and I hugged her.

'We just don't want to see you hurt again, Pip. Nell and I have seen you hurt too many times before.'

'I appreciate it. And you will never know how much I value your friendship and advice. Plus the fact that you both gave up your lives to take on this project with me. But I've healed since we've been here. I can't explain it. Maybe it's because it's where I grew up. And Aunty Vi made me see that I could be loved. Maybe it's simply because I'm back in the islands where I love to be. Maybe it's because I'm doing something with meaning. And that I love doing it. But honestly, Tam, I'm happy.'

'And Rafe?'

'Yeah, I think he's cute. Well, okay, he's as sexy as hell. That voice and those eyes, but I'm not going to rush into anything. Without breaching his confidence, he's been hurt too, and he's healing. He's also focused on writing his next book, so whatever ideas you've got, we are friends. Good friends, close friends, and that's the way it will stay for the time being.'

Tam smiled at me before she picked up the spoon off the sink. 'For the time being?'

'Yes,' I said. 'For the time being. I've got a resort to open.'
##

Rafe was walking beside me as we made our way to the bay, and

Tam raised her eyebrows with a secret smile as he took my arm to help me over one of the fallen tree trunks that was still across the path.

I turned and pulled a face at her. 'Behave,' I mouthed silently. It was like being a teenager again, and I was loving getting to know him more each day.

Today was a red-letter day. The material for the huts had been delivered, and the workmen had arrived to build the timber floors. The hut frames were modular, and we were going to erect them ourselves. We'd planned a sunset drink on the beach to celebrate.

'Are you sure we can do it?' Nell asked for at least the tenth time as we stood at the edge of the sand and watched the joists get nailed onto the frame of the first hut. 'Don't we need a carpenter?'

'Of course, we can do it,' Evie said in her husky voice. She'd fitted into our household as I'd known she would, and her plans for the gardens and the tracks to the various bays and Red Wave Wall—yes, Rafe had given us permission to cross his land—were well under way. I reached over and squeezed his hand.

His face lit up in that beautiful smile of his, and my stomach took a tumble.

'What was that for?'

'Just a thank you.'

'No need. I'm happy to be here. You—all of you, I mean'—he glanced at Tam— 'have made my life on the island a joy.'

Tam pretended to gag, but there was a grin on her face as she went over to stand beside Nell and Evie to watch the two workmen.

'Just ignore her,' I said. The

noise of the hammering was overpowering, and I gestured to the bay. We walked down to the edge of the water together.

'What's wrong with Tam? Does it bother her that I spend so much time over here? Maybe you'd better come over and visit me more often, Pip?' Rafe's eyes held mine and my stomach did that tumble again. I had trouble reading him. He was the consummate gentleman. Always polite to each of us, but sometimes there was something in the way he looked at me. Even if there was something there, like I told Tam, I wasn't ready for it. I wanted to find myself, and see my plans come to fruition before I made any moves in that direction.

'Is that an invitation? For some reason my voice was husky like Evie's and I cleared my throat.

Okay, so even if I wasn't ready for those moves, I could still flirt.

'It is.'

I didn't object when Rafe slung his arm around my shoulder as we looked over the water. Spring was not far off, and the water was a deep translucent blue. White sails dotted the passage and a tourist launch full of backpackers hooted its horn as it motored past our bay.

'It's so peaceful here,' I whispered half to myself.

'It is.' We stood in a companionable silence watching the water until Evie called out.

'Come and see, guys.'

We walked back to the others to see the first floor had been laid. I had designed it with Evie's help so that the hut was a hexagonal shape, with a small porch overlooking the bay.

Rafe left me at the path. He

brushed a kiss across my cheek, obviously not concerned by the look of delight on Tam's face. 'Would you like to come over when you finish work for the day? I've got a bottle of white chilling in the wine fridge,' he whispered.

I smiled and pretended to misunderstand. 'All of us?' I asked cheekily.

'No, Pippa. Just you.'

'I'm sorry. Tonight, we've planned a drink to celebrate what we've achieved so far. A girls' night.'

His face fell, and he straightened up. 'Very well. It's past time I was back at work anyway.'

I grabbed his arm and moved closer to him. 'But if that invitation stands, I'd love to take it up tomorrow night.'

His smile was wide. 'Oh yes, it

will stand for as long as you want it to. I can wait.'

I could hear him whistling as he headed back to his house on the hill.

Epilogue

Pippa

A bottle of bubbles didn't last long between four when there was a celebration underway. The floors of the first four huts had been laid today, and now we were ready to put up the modular buildings. The frames were stacked waiting for us to begin work tomorrow.

I lifted my glass in a toast. 'To Ma Carmichael's Place.'

'To Ma's,' my three friends chimed in.

We clinked glasses and sipped our champagne.

We were sitting on the sand looking across the bay to the peak that marked the centre of the island. Evie and Nell had gone for a quick swim while they'd waited for Tam and I to come down with the bubbles and the glasses. The sun was warm as spring approached and we all wore our straw hats.

'I think, ladies, when we get the interiors of the huts done, we might set an opening date and work towards that. What do you think of that?'

'Super,' Nell said.

Tam giggled. 'You're getting an English accent too. Or the lingo, at least.'

Nell nudged her and Tam's glass tipped a little.

'Hey watch it, I'll spill my bubbles!'

Evie laughed with them. 'It's just like being back at uni, being here on the island with you lot. No cares, no worries, no pressure.'

I rolled my eyes. 'No, just a resort under development, a huge landscaping project'—I nodded at Evie—'and a big accounting task underway, thanks to Nell, and an outdoor restaurant and exciting menus to be planned.' I raised my glass. 'Thank you, my friends.'

'That's right.' Tam nodded. 'Just like Evie said. No cares, no worries, no pressure.'

'And let's keep it that way. I want to propose another toast.' I lifted my glass. 'To friendship, girls. To the unbreakable bond that has seen us stay together through the ups and downs of life. And boy, there's been some of them over the past ten years.'

'To friendship,' they chorused.

As the sun slipped slowly towards the sea, we sat there in silence. Four women who cared for and looked out for each other. When the bubbles were finished, we put our glasses down and looped our arms around each other's shoulders. The sky faded from that deep indigo blue into an array of pinks shot with gold, and the only sound was the small waves breaking on the shingly sand.

I smiled as a light came on up the hill and Rafe's silhouette appeared at the window as he looked down to the bay.

Our bay.

He wouldn't be able to see us, but I could see him. I was beside Tam and I felt her tense as she leaned forward.

'Pip, what's that?'

I pulled my gaze away from Rafe's house and looked in the direction she was pointing. 'What?'

'There's something in the water. Look just out at the point. Something black.'

'A shark?' Nell shuddered. 'We were just swimming out there before you came down.'

'No.' Tam jumped to her feet

and we watched as she ran down to the water.

I stood and held out my hand to pull Nell up.

'I think it's a person,' Tam called back to us. 'I'm going to go out to the point.'

It was too dark to see clearly, and I couldn't imagine that Tam was right. There were no boats in sight, and no lights, unless there was a boat around the point in Back Bay. Even so it was too late at night for someone to be in the water. I wouldn't even swim in the daytime; I was worried about the shark attacks a couple of years ago and was very wary.

When the business could afford it, I intended to put a pool in, adjacent to the outdoor restaurant.

And a jacuzzi, and a day spa. My thoughts went into planning mode as we followed Tam out onto the rocky point. It was too dark to see, but the closer we got to the water, the more I could hear splashing in the water.

'Could be dolphins,' I said.

Tam yelled as we were almost to her. 'It's a person, and I think they're in trouble.' As we took off towards her, she threw her straw hat to the ground, pulled her dress over her head and stepped into the water. Before we could reach her, she was swimming out into the bay.

'Tam, don't be stupid,' I yelled, reaching for her hat as the wind picked it up.

I looked around quickly. We were at the opposite end of the bay to the jetty, and by the time I could run over and start the launch, she could be back in.

But nevertheless, I remained poised to run as Nell picked up

Tam's dress and hat.

I stared at the water and it was only a minute or two later that the splashing reached us followed by Tam's voice. She sounded out of breath.

'I've got them. I'll swim into the beach. It'll be easier than getting out on the rocks.'

I half held my breath as we raced around to the beach and waited for Tam to appear. By the time we got there I was breathless, and Nell was close to tears.

'Oh, Pip, is she going to make it?' she cried.

Gradually we could make out a disturbance in the water and I prayed under my breath that she would get in safely.

Suddenly there was a huge splash, and Tam appeared in front of us. She was dragging a person by the armpits and we all hurried into the water to help her.

It was a woman. She was wearing a long white dress and it clung to her legs, impeding her progress. We each put our hands beneath her and carried her into the shore.

'Are you okay, Tam?' I glanced over at my brave friend. I was in awe of her bravery. There was no way I could have done that.

'I'm fine. I think she is too. She was swimming by herself, but I think she passed out when I reached her.

We lay the woman on her side in the recovery position, and I was relieved when she coughed and groaned. It was almost too dark to see.

'Evie, Nell, run up to the house and get a blanket and some water,' I said as I bent down with Tam.

The woman was breathing on

her own, and as I watched her eyes flickered open.

'Thank you,' she whispered.

'Are you all right? Can you breathe okay? Are you hurt anywhere?' Tam fired questions at her and the woman nodded.

'I'm okay. Thank you.' Her voice was stronger, and she tried to sit up. 'Please help me sit up, it'll be easier to catch my breath.'

Her voice had a slight accent that I couldn't place, and her dark hair was plastered to her skull in wet ringlets. Her eyes were dark and wide.

Tam and I supported her as she sat up on the sand.

'What's your name?' I asked.

'Eliza.' Her voice was faint.

'How did you get in the water?' Tam asked.

She looked us both blankly. 'I don't know.'

THE END

Eliza's story is available in large print also. Email Annie to reserve a print copy: annie@annieseaton.net

Come and spend some more time with the girls on Pentecost Island...see if Pippa and Rafe develop their friendship to something deeper, and see if Tam, Nell and Evie are happy to stay on the island. And Eliza? Well . .

Eliza Pengelly has always led the life she wanted, but sometimes poor choices lead to heartbreak.
*   The final choice–and the biggest mistake of her life—sees her fleeing to Pentecost Island. Desperate to make a fresh start, Eliza is happy to work—and hide— on the island for as long as Pippa*

needs a carpenter to achieve her dream. Having friends around to support her through tough times is a bonus.

But Eliza quickly learns you can't outrun your demons. The arrival of charismatic sailor, Phillipe Renton threatens the safety of the new life Eliza is creating.

Living his life on the oceans and travelling the world, Phillipe doesn't do relationships, but the attraction to vulnerable Eliza is impossible to resist.

Will her dark secret be revealed—a secret that could destroy any chance of happiness for her new life?

Also by Annie Seaton

Whitsunday Dawn
Undara
Porter Sisters Series
   Kakadu Sunset
   Daintree
   Diamond Sky
   Hidden Valley Sunrise (2020)
Pentecost Island Series (2020)
Pippa
Eliza
Nell
Tamsin
Evie
More to come in 2021
Bondi Beach Love Series
Beach House
Beach Music
Beach Walk
Beach Dreams
Prickle Creek Series
Her Outback Cowboy
Her Outback Surprise

His Outback Nanny
His Outback Temptation
Second Chance Bay Series
Her Outback Playboy
Her Outback Protector
Her Outback Haven
Her Outback Paradise
Love Across Time Series
Come Back to Me
Follow Me
Lucy's Story (2020)
Half Moon Bay Series
Tangling with the CEO
Brushing Off the Boss
Guarding His Heart
The Trouble with Paradise
Deadly Secrets
Adventures in Time
Silver Valley Witch
The Emerald Necklace
Ten Days in Tuscany
Worth the Wait
Full Circle

ACKNOWLEDGEMENTS

A special thank you to:
my wonderful editor and critique
partner, Susanne Bellamy,
and my eagle-eyed proof-reader,
Roby Aiken.

About the Author

Author of the Year Ausrom Readers' Choice 2014

Best Established Author Ausrom Readers' Choice 2015

Finalist for Author of the Year, Book of the Year, Cover of the Year, Ausrom Readers' Choice 2016

Best Established Author, Ausrom Readers' Choice 2017

Book of the Year (Whitsunday Dawn) Ausrom Readers' Choice

Awards 2018

Annie lives in Australia, on the beautiful north coast of New South Wales. She sits in her writing chair and looks out over the tranquil Pacific Ocean. She has fulfilled her lifelong dream of becoming an author and is producing books at a prolific rate.

She writes contemporary romance and loves telling the stories that always have a happily ever after. She lives with her very own hero of many years and they share their home with Toby, the naughtiest dog in the universe, and Barney, the rag doll kitten, who hides when the grandchildren come to visit.

Stay up to date with her latest releases on her website and store: http://www.annieseaton.net

If you would like to stay up to date with Annie's releases, subscribe to her newsletter on her website.